A HEATHER PARKER ORIGINAL

KAY CORRELL

This book is dedicated to all the people who love their creative pursuits—be it drawing, writing, photography, crafts, or the many other creative outlets we escape into.

Heather Parker has stayed home in Moonbeam longer than she ever thought possible. Which makes it really hard to keep avoiding Jesse…

Eventually they come to a mutual truce.

… and then a bit more.

But a surprise from the past threatens everything. Secrets come tumbling out and everyone is shocked by what Heather has hidden from them. From Jesse. From her cousin. From her mother.

A secret that threatens to tear apart Heather's relationship with everyone she cares about.

Continue on in the Moonbeam Bay series and see what the Parker women are up to. And just how many more secrets does this family have?

KAY'S BOOKS

Find more information on all my books at
kaycorrell.com

COMFORT CROSSING ~ THE SERIES

The Shop on Main - Book One
The Memory Box - Book Two
The Christmas Cottage - A Holiday Novella
(Book 2.5)
The Letter - Book Three
The Christmas Scarf - A Holiday Novella
(Book 3.5)
The Magnolia Cafe - Book Four
The Unexpected Wedding - Book Five

The Wedding in the Grove - (a crossover short story between series - with Josephine and Paul from The Letter.)

LIGHTHOUSE POINT ~ THE SERIES

Wish Upon a Shell - Book One
Wedding on the Beach - Book Two
Love at the Lighthouse - Book Three
Cottage near the Point - Book Four
Return to the Island - Book Five
Bungalow by the Bay - Book Six

CHARMING INN ~ Return to Lighthouse Point

One Simple Wish - Book One
Two of a Kind - Book Two
Three Little Things - Book Three
Four Short Weeks - Book Four
Five Years or So - Book Five
Six Hours Away - Book Six
Charming Christmas - Book Seven

SWEET RIVER ~ THE SERIES

A Dream to Believe in - Book One

A Memory to Cherish - Book Two

A Song to Remember - Book Three

A Time to Forgive - Book Four

A Summer of Secrets - Book Five

A Moment in the Moonlight - Book Six

MOONBEAM BAY ~ THE SERIES (2021)

The Parker Women - Book One

The Parker Cafe - Book Two

A Heather Parker Original - Book Three

The Parker Family Secret - Book Four

Grace Parker's Peach Pie - Book Five

The Perks of Being a Parker - Book Six

INDIGO BAY ~ A multi-author sweet romance series

Sweet Days by the Bay - Kay's Complete Collection of stories in the Indigo Bay series

Or buy them separately:

Sweet Sunrise - Book Three

Sweet Holiday Memories - A short holiday story

Sweet Starlight - Book Nine

Sign up for my newsletter at my website *kaycorrell.com* to make sure you don't miss any new releases or sales.

CHAPTER 1

Heather Parker sat in the shade of the gazebo on the beach, a sketch pad in hand. A young mother and her daughter knelt in the sand, making a sandcastle. The girl, who looked to be about three years old, concentrated on carefully decorating the castle with seashells.

Heather looked down and began to sketch the scene. The mother, the girl, the sandcastle, the waves. The familiarity of the act of sketching warmed her from the inside like the sunshine warmed her skin. It had been a while. She'd been busy helping her mother move and helping out at Sea Glass Cafe. Her illustrations had taken a back seat to her family obligations.

At least until her agent called and asked to see new work. A card company was interested in her designing a line of greeting cards for them with a beachy theme. Perfect timing since she was here in Moonbeam with daily access to the beach. She wanted to see if she could get some preliminary sketches done to show the company.

A shriek drew her attention away from the sketch and back to the beach. A wave had come up with the rising tide and knocked down the sandcastle. The little girl launched herself into her mother's arms, sobbing. The mother held the child and patted her back. As the girl finally calmed down, the woman wiped away her tears and took her hand. They moved further up the beach and began the process of building the castle again.

Heather's heart clutched in her chest at the tenderness of the moment. The closeness that was obvious between the mother and child. That was not something she'd really had growing up, and a part of her, deep inside, was still a small girl longing for it. She sighed and went back to work.

She continued her sketch, glancing up now and then to take in more details. She concentrated on the sketch, lost in her own little world where she got to create the reality she wanted on the page. She liked that. Creating the scene, changing things, the total control over the perfect little vignettes. If only life were that easy to control.

A shadow fell across her page and she looked up. Her heart thumped, and she caught her breath. "Jesse."

No, life was *not* easy to control.

"Heather. I thought that was you." Jesse stood right in front of her looking unbelievably handsome in worn shorts and a t-shirt stretched tightly across his broad chest.

"I was just sketching." That much was obvious. Still, Jesse had a way of making her thoughts jumble and words come out awkwardly.

"Didn't know if you'd just jump up and run off if I stopped to say hi." He cocked his head to one side, eyeing her.

"I... of course not." Although, that had been her first instinct. And it still did seem like the safest choice...

He glanced at her drawing pad, then out toward the beach. A small smile flitted across his face. "You always did like to draw those scenes with all the tiny details."

She set her pencil down. "It's just a rough sketch."

Jesse turned back to her. "So Parker Cafe seems to be doing well. I heard you've been helping out."

"Sea Glass Cafe," she corrected automatically.

He laughed. "Yes, Sea Glass. I should remember that if I run into Livy."

"My cousin spends half her time correcting people." She let a small smile creep across her lips. Who knew she could make small talk with Jesse?

"I'm glad that it's working out for Livy. And for your mom. I hear rave reviews of her cooking there."

"She's got all the family's old recipes. And she really is a great cook." Heather wished she would have gotten the cooking gene from her mom, but no such luck.

"So—" Jesse paused, looking tentative. "How have you been?"

"Fine."

"You've stuck around Moonbeam longer than your usual stay."

So he'd been keeping track of her comings

and goings? "Well—there's the cafe. And then Mom…"

"I heard your folks are divorcing."

"It's a done deal now."

"Oh." He looked surprised.

"Mom didn't want it dragging out any longer. She just moved out from Aunt Donna's house to her own apartment, too."

"Did she?"

"She's never lived alone, and I honestly think she's looking forward to it." Why was she telling him all of this?

"Good for her. I hope she enjoys her independence."

She didn't bother to or want to tell him that her mother walked out of the divorce without any money and that her father had taken everything. That wasn't hers to tell.

"So are you going to stick around while she gets adjusted to her new life?"

"I am. For a bit, anyway."

"Maybe I'll run into you again. Or—you could come on The Destiny one night. Have dinner. See the sunset. Ask Livy to join you. Or your Mom," he offered with a bit of a hopeful look in his eyes.

"I—I'm not sure. Maybe." Definitely not.

"Okay, well, I'll see you soon." There was a hint of sadness in his eyes as he turned and started to walk away. He pivoted back to face her. "And it was nice talking to you. You know… not arguing. Or you hurrying off."

"I don't hurry off," she insisted, knowing full well that she did.

He just tossed her a grin and walked away down the beach.

That was probably the most civil conversation she'd had with Jesse Brown in years. And she wasn't sure if that was good or bad.

Evelyn stood in the kitchen at Sea Glass Cafe. She was in her element here in this treasured space. She loved baking and cooking and trying new recipes. She loved the kitchen filled with sumptuous aromas that swirled around her as she worked. And much to her delight, the customers seemed to really enjoy her food. Her niece, Livy, said the cafe was already turning a profit. She was proud she was playing a part in that.

The lunch rush was over, and she paged

through the recipe binder, trying to decide what kind of pastry to make for tomorrow. Maybe some peach pies. The customers seemed to love Grace Parker's peach pie recipe. Actually, they loved all of the old family recipes.

Though Livy technically ran the cafe, she had given Evelyn complete control over the daily menu. She made cinnamon rolls for the breakfast crowd most mornings along with chocolate-filled donuts and breakfast sandwiches with eggs and bacon. In addition to regular items the customers could depend on, she also tried out new specials of the day. She'd never worked so hard in her life or put in such long hours... and she'd never been this happy.

A person would think a recently divorced woman whose husband had left her for a new young woman wouldn't be this happy. But she was. And content. She whistled under her breath as she leafed through the recipes. Oh, here was a good one. Pumpkin scones. Hm, pumpkin scones or peach pies...

Her sister, Donna, breezed into the kitchen with a tray of dirty dishes. "Collected these on my way through the dining room." She set the dishes by the dishwasher. "Big lunch crowd today."

"It was."

"It's because Mondays are known for your pot pies." Donna smiled. "And then a lot of the customers wander through Parker's General Store. I swear, I thought Olivia was a bit crazy with the whole building expansion and cafe plan, but it was a great idea. Business at Parker's has really picked up."

"That's because it's not so crammed in every space now. It really looks darling, like an old-fashioned general store." Evelyn motioned to a stool by the counter. "Want some coffee?"

"Sure, I've got some time." Donna perched on the stool.

Evelyn poured them both a cup and sat by her sister. Relief flushed through her at getting off her feet for a bit. A tiny break wouldn't hurt.

"I miss having you living with me." Donna took a sip of her coffee. "I'd gotten used to having someone in the house all the time again."

"You mean you miss me bringing home dinner from the cafe." Evelyn smiled.

"That, too."

"But now you have more privacy when Barry comes over to visit."

"True, but you weren't ever in the way."

But she'd felt in the way. Kind of. Plus, she'd been so ready to live on her own. Eager to have her own place and prove to herself she didn't need to depend on anyone but herself. She took a sip of her coffee and changed the subject. "How's Barry's new job going?"

"Great. He said the plans for converting the old hotel near Naples are coming along. He drives down there most days, but comes home every night."

"So he extended his rental on the house next to yours?"

"Yes, the Meyers were thrilled to have him rent longer."

"I'm glad all that's working out for you."

"I do like seeing him all the time. We have dinner most nights, or at least a drink out on the point if he or I come home late."

"I miss sitting out on the point with you and watching the sunset." Evelyn sighed.

"You should come over one night."

"I will. Soon. Right now I can't wait to get home each night and settle into my own place."

"Did you ever get a table and chairs?"

"I did. At the thrift shop in town. It was pretty beat up, but Heather painted it with chalk paint. It's a pretty teal color now and fits in great with the plans I have for the apartment. It's starting to slowly come together. I'm having so much fun making it just how I want it."

"With no one telling you what you can or can't do." Donna frowned slightly. "Any more problems with your ex?"

"Haven't heard a word from him. Not since the divorce was finalized."

"Is he still with that Lacey person?"

"I don't really know, and luckily I haven't run into him recently." And she hoped that streak continued. The less she saw of him, the better. They didn't run in the same circles anymore. She'd been dropped from the country club membership, and none of her supposed friends from the club had reached out to her. They'd thrown their allegiance to Darren and cut her from their ranks. Which was fine, really. Who needed fake friends?

"Anyway, so I hear Melody is helping out with the cooking here at the cafe more?" Donna set down her cup. "You really need to cut back on your hours some. You work all the time."

Evelyn laughed. "You're one to talk. You work long hours six days a week. And I know you pop into the store on Sundays sometimes, too."

"What can I say? I love owning Parker's and running the store. Chatting with the customers. Even setting up new displays. Most days the hours just fly by."

"We're pretty lucky, aren't we?"

"We're *very* lucky," Donna agreed.

Livy hurried into the kitchen and up to Donna. "Mom, I have the *best* idea."

Donna looked at her daughter warily. "What idea? I'm just getting comfortable with your *last* idea. I'm not a very big fan of change."

Evelyn chuckled at Donna's understatement.

CHAPTER 2

Olivia laughed at her mother. "No, you don't like change. I'm well aware of that. We all are. But this won't be as big of a change as the expansion."

Her mother sighed. "Hit me while I'm in a good mood. Evie and I were just saying how lucky we are."

She sucked in a deep breath, hoping her mother would like her plan. "Okay... so you know how the upstairs floor here in this building is mostly storage? How about we make it into a seasonal room? You know. Like Easter, and Halloween, and Christmas? I think we could even keep up a portion of it with Christmas things all year. You know how the tourists seem to like to get little Christmas ornaments and gifts to remind them of their trips to Moonbeam."

"I—" Her mother paused, then a tentative smile spread across her face. "I think that's a marvelous idea."

"You do?" She'd been expecting a lot of resistance to the idea.

"I think it's a great idea, too. And when the cafe has a waitlist, the customers can go upstairs and browse around," Evelyn said.

"Ever since Emily installed that texting program for our waitlist, the customers really have been browsing around while they wait." Olivia was amazed at all her daughter had learned this year about software and so much techie stuff. Stuff she, herself, was *not* that great at.

"You're lucky Austin has had time to teach Emily so much," Evelyn said. "Speaking of Austin. How is he? I haven't seen him come into the cafe in the last week or so."

"He's been busy. He was out of town visiting a client, but he'll be back tonight." And she couldn't wait to see him. She missed him when he took business trips. She'd gotten quite used to seeing him most days, something she never thought would happen. Olivia Foster had a boyfriend. And a serious one at that.

"You should take off early then," Evelyn insisted. "Melody and I have things covered here at the cafe. And Brittany will be in too, to wait tables."

"I don't know. I feel guilty leaving you with the dinner rush."

"Nonsense. Go home. Get ready. Have a nice evening with Austin."

"If you're sure." She still wavered, but it did sound enticing.

"Go." Evelyn fluttered her hands, swishing her away.

"Okay, okay. I'm leaving." She turned to her mother. "And I'll show you the plans for the seasonal room tomorrow, okay?"

"Sounds good." Her mother nodded.

She hurried out of the kitchen, straightening a few chairs as she passed through the cafe. With a small smile, she headed home, anxious to see Austin.

Austin sent a text to Livy as soon as he got home. He'd rented a small cottage on the beach with a marvelous deck overlooking the gulf. It suited him perfectly. Almost *everything* these days suited him perfectly. His relationship with Livy. His work. This cottage.

Livy answered his text immediately and told him she'd taken the night off. That was an unexpected bonus. They made plans to meet at his cottage and then decide what they were going to do.

After a brief shower to wash off the travel grime, he quickly picked up the cottage, though it didn't need much. He didn't really have much here. His computer and work things. He'd bought some casual clothing to wear here since he didn't own much warm weather clothing. It was kind of silly to be renting two places, one in Colorado and one here, but he wasn't ready to leave Moonbeam. Not just yet.

Occasionally he thought that maybe he'd let the Colorado condo go and move here, but he didn't think he and Livy were quite at that stage yet. So renting two places was his best compromise.

He answered the door as soon as Livy knocked, and a sense of rightness settled over him, washing away the longing he'd felt from being away from her. He pulled her into his arms and kissed her. "I've been wanting to do that all week."

She smiled up at him. "And I've been waiting for you to do that."

He took her hand. It felt small and delicate, mixed with strong. An eclectic mix like so much about Livy. "Come in." He led her inside. "So, have you decided what we should do tonight?"

"Kiss?" Her lips tilted into a teasing smile.

"Okay, we could do that." He tugged her back into his arms and kissed her again. And once more.

She laughed and finally pulled away. "Though, I guess we should do something more than stand here kissing all night."

"I don't know. I'm pretty good with the kissing plan."

"We could go out to Jimmy's for dinner," she suggested.

"Or we could stay in and I wouldn't have to share you."

"There is that whole dinner thing, though." She playfully poked him in the chest.

"Luckily I picked up groceries on the way in town." He tapped his forehead. "I'm smart like that."

"You mean you thought I'd be working late

tonight, and you'd have to make dinner for yourself."

"Okay, that, too. But I have plenty. Want to split a steak? And I have some potatoes I can throw in to bake. And we'll make a salad."

"That sounds wonderful. A night in away from people? Perfect."

"Why don't you go out on the deck and relax? I'll throw the potatoes in and grab us a couple of beers." Her favorite local craft beer, of course, because it was now his favorite, too.

She wandered out onto the deck, and he hurried with his preparations. He joined her shortly, and they clinked beer bottles before taking a sip.

"Ah, this is so good. I'm glad you introduced me to it."

"I do like an ice-cold beer on a hot summer day." She pressed the bottle to her lips and took another sip.

His gaze lingered on her lips for a moment and heat surged through him.

Which he ignored.

Luckily there was a breeze coming in from the gulf. That would surely help...

They settled onto a wooden loveseat and he

draped his arm around her shoulder, pulling her close to him.

She leaned her head on his shoulder. "I'm right where I want to be."

And with her words, his heart beat stronger. He was right where he wanted to be, too. Who knew his decision to vacation on Moonbeam Bay and visit his old friend Jesse Brown would make such a difference in his life? Best decision he'd ever made.

CHAPTER 3

Heather waited patiently at Brewster's the next morning for Livy to join her. She had Livy's steaming cup of coffee waiting. They'd both been so busy that they hadn't met for coffee in weeks, and she missed their morning get-togethers.

She took a sip of her coffee and looked out across Moonbeam Bay. A large sailboat was under motor, headed out to the gulf for a day of sailing. A few fishing boats cruised past on their way to their favorite fishing spots. She took her iPad out of her purse and switched on the sketching program and quickly sketched her surroundings. A couple sitting at a nearby table, holding hands while they sipped their coffee, an old golden retriever with a gray face settled by their feet. A lone man typing away on his laptop, ignoring the wonderful view beside him.

As usual, she got lost in her sketch and the world she was creating.

Livy slid into the seat across from her and broke the spell.

"Morning." She turned off her tablet and slid it back into her purse.

"Whatcha working on?" Livy asked.

"Oh, just sketching the people."

"So do you like working digitally on that iPad or the old-fashioned way on paper?"

"I don't know. Both, I guess." It had taken her a while to convert to doing some of her art digitally, but she enjoyed it now. She just considered it a different medium. Like watercolor, or colored pencils, or simple pencil sketching. Always something a bit different.

"So I talked to Mom about adding the seasonal room to Parker's."

Heather raised an eyebrow. "And how did that go? Aunt Donna isn't big on change."

Livy laughed. "She's not. But she was surprisingly positive about this suggestion. I'm going to head up to the storage room today and see how much work it will be to clear out some of the stuff. There's a back room we could still use for storage, but the front room has those big windows overlooking Magnolia Avenue. All that nice light coming in? I think it will be perfect and airy."

"I can help you set up the displays," Heather offered.

Livy smiled. "I was hoping you'd offer. You've got such a great eye for that. I thought we'd have a Christmas area, then whatever season is coming up, we'll have displays for that."

"My hat's off to you, Livy. You've done such a great job expanding Parker's. And the cafe is a roaring success. I'm proud of you, cuz."

"I'm kind of proud of me, too. I never thought Mom would let me do so much with Parker's. And the cafe turning a profit so quickly? I'm thrilled. I've hired extra help now that it appears we're going to stay busy. At least I hope we do."

"I wish I could convince Mom to take more time off. I think she's worried about finances though. I told her I could help her out, but she insists she wants to do this all on her own."

"To be honest, I'm thinking of making her part owner of the cafe. She can have a slice of the profits along with her salary. I mean, she's the reason it's so successful. Her cooking. Her recipes. It just seems like part of the profits should be hers. Besides, Parker's really is a family business, and if she wants to work at it, she deserves part of the profits."

Heather looked at her cousin in surprise. "Really? She'll be thrilled. I know she has thrown her whole heart into the cafe. She loves working there."

"I'm going to talk to Mom about it today. I'm sure she'll be fine with it. I mean, Parker's is a family business. And you invested in the cafe, too. I've already made up a payment schedule to pay you back."

"There's no rush on that."

"But I want to. I'm grateful you had enough faith in me to invest in the cafe and help me get it started."

"I wanted to." Heather grinned. "But I have to admit, I'm kind of glad you've hired more help. I wasn't cut out to be a waitress for long."

Livy's laugh rang out. "No, you weren't. But we sure appreciated all the help you gave us."

"I'm still willing to fill in sometimes if you need help... notice the *sometimes*."

"Duly noted." Livy took a sip of her coffee. "I've missed meeting you here. Talking to you. I feel like all we do is exchange a few words in passing at the cafe."

"I was just thinking the same thing. Maybe we could even take a night and do something? Go out to dinner? Though I know you're busy at the cafe and with Austin."

"I'm never too busy for you. Let's do dinner. You know, I've been wanting to go on Jesse's dinner cruise."

"Oh, I was thinking more like Jimmy's." The last thing she needed was to run into Jesse again.

"Aren't you the least bit curious to see what Jesse has done to The Destiny?"

"I'm sure it's nice. It's just..."

"You still haven't talked to him and worked things out, have you?" Livy rolled her eyes. "That's just silly. You guys were such good friends."

"Were being the operative word. We've just moved on. But for your information, I did talk to him yesterday. He saw me out sketching by the beach."

"You did?" Livy's eyes widened. "How did that go?"

"It was... fine." Heather sighed. "Really, just a bit of chitchat."

"And did you run off as soon as he showed up?"

"No, I didn't. *He* actually left after we talked."

"So you think things are better between you now? It would be really cool to hang out with you and Jesse and Austin." Livy's eyes brightened.

"Oh, I don't know." Icy panic washed over her just thinking about seeing Jesse. It was best to just avoid him. She could be civil. Friendly, even. But not *friends*.

"What if we all went on The Destiny? Wouldn't that be fun? I'm sure Jesse could find some time to hang out with us on the cruise."

"No. Really, Liv. Just... no."

She sighed. "Well, I tried."

"You did." The panic began to subside when Livy finally conceded to her wishes.

"Then how about Jimmy's on Thursday night? Just you and me," Livy suggested.

"That sounds great."

"About seven? I'll get things situated at the cafe and meet you there? Both Emily and Brittany are working Thursday night along with the new worker I hired."

"Jimmy's on Thursday. It's a date."

CHAPTER 4

On Thursday, as planned, Heather headed to Jimmy's. She waved to Livy and went to join her at a harborside table. "You beat me," Heather said as she slipped into the seat across from Livy.

"I know. Doesn't happen often. You're always early."

They ordered drinks and Heather pretended to look at the menu. They both had it memorized, so a menu was frivolous, but she couldn't decide what sounded good tonight. Fish tacos? Grouper sandwich? Or maybe a big salad with shrimp...

"Heather, look. There's Austin and Jesse."

Heather glanced toward the doorway. Great. "Did you plan this?"

"No, of course not." But Livy's face didn't look very convincing.

The men walked up to them. Jesse looking surprised to see them, Austin, not so much. "Well, hello. This a surprise," Austin said, trying to look credible.

She shot Livy a look. Livy sent back an overly innocent expression, turned, and smiled at the men. "Do you two want to join us? We haven't ordered yet."

"We don't want to intrude," Jesse said.

"Oh, you aren't. We'd love for you to join us. Right, Heather?"

Heather glared at Livy. "Yes, love it," she lied.

Austin sat next to Livy so, of course, that only left the seat next to her for Jesse. He promptly claimed it, and she ignored how close he was. The men ordered drinks while Heather concentrated on the menu. Concentrated hard. Read every little detail and noticed they had a typo in mayonnaise. One n. Maybe she should get up and go talk to Jimmy and tell him...

Austin and Livy chatted about their days, oblivious to the silence across the table from them. Or maybe they knew it was there but ignored it. They all ordered. Heather decided on the salad with shrimp but ordered a side of hushpuppies to split with Livy. Might as well have some carbs to tone down her stress level. Maybe she'd even finish her meal with key lime pie. Why not?

"Heather picked up another greeting card line," Livy offered up in a lull in the conversation.

"You did?" Austin asked.

"I did. For a line of beach-themed cards."

"That sounds nice." Austin smiled at her. "So you do all the drawings and they add words, or it's just cards with drawings?"

"This company adds the words. They've actually sent me some of the wording, so I'll draw according to the sayings. And they want some of my other illustrations, too. If the line does well, they'll expand to putting it on coasters, t-shirts, tote bags. Things like that."

"You have a very interesting career." Austin shot a look at Jesse.

Jesse, who still hadn't said a word since he sat down.

"How's The Destiny doing, Jesse?" Livy tried again to jumpstart the conversation.

"Fine. Busy. No complaints."

"Heather and I were talking about going on

a dinner cruise," Livy said. Or, more appropriately, lied.

She kicked Livy under the table.

"Oh, that would be fun. We should all go. Jesse, you could take some time to chat with us if we go on a cruise, couldn't you? Maybe grab dinner with us?" Austin asked.

"I... uh... sure." He looked about as ambushed as she felt.

"Great, how about next Monday? I know that Livy is busy with the cafe on the weekend," Austin suggested.

Heather struggled to come up with a reason she couldn't go, but nothing seemed plausible. Maybe she'd just have to be sick on Monday.

"Monday works," Jesse said. "It will actually be a great day for me to do it. I have some extra help that night. Training a few more employees this week and they'll be there."

"Great, Monday it is. Right, Heather?" Livy insisted.

Heather nodded, still ignoring the fact that Jesse sat right next to her. And he seemed to be starting to relax. That wasn't fair. Why couldn't she?

"Austin said that you got the new ordering system for Parker's—I mean, Sea Glass Cafe—

up and running," Jesse said as he leaned back, relaxed. So very relaxed.

"We did. It's a bit different. We have to juggle online orders along with the in-person orders. But it's working out. And our business really took off when we added it. We hired another part-time cook, as well as another server." Livy grinned. "Because Heather was so done with being a waitress."

"It wasn't so bad," she insisted, then smiled. "Well, it kinda was. But I'm glad to be back to my own work. Especially with this new card line."

Their meals came, and much to Heather's surprise, her tension began to dissipate. She was able to sit back in her chair, her spine no longer frozen ramrod straight. Just a simple dinner with friends. That wasn't so bad, was it?

"You know, I wonder if your mother could help me plan out some new menus for The Destiny. I feel like I'm stuck on just a few dinner buffets that I rotate through." Jesse looked at her. "You think she'd do that?" He turned to Livy. "Though, nothing to compete with the cafe, of course."

"Probably," Heather said.

"I'd pay her, of course. For the planning and

providing recipes. And... you think maybe she'd train the cook on them?"

"Ask her. I bet she would." Her mother was always looking for other gigs to add to her income.

"Great. I'll talk to her this week."

Livy looked at her watch. "Oh, it's getting late. I'm working the early shift tomorrow. I should go."

"I'll walk you home." Austin jumped up and nodded at Jesse.

"I'll walk Heather home," Jesse said without actually asking her.

"You don't need to. I'll be fine."

"But... I want to," he insisted.

"Uh, ah, okay." Nice answer. So well-spoken. She rolled her eyes at herself as she stood.

"Heather, can't we talk? I hate how things are between us now." Jesse paused under a streetlamp on their walk to her condo.

"What do you mean? We got along fine tonight, didn't we?" Though she'd been as tense as a strung guitar for the first half of the evening.

Jesse let out a sigh. "Please? Let's talk. Come on." He captured her hand in his—which it took all her self-control not to snatch back—and led her over to a bench at the edge of the harbor walk.

She sat down beside him, her hand thankfully out of his now. She stared down at it resting in her lap. At her nail polish. At a silver ring with a turquoise stone on her pinkie finger and a silver bracelet encircling her wrist. If she concentrated on these tiny details...

Her heart hammered in her chest, her pulse throbbing so hard that she could barely hear him when he started talking again.

"I'm sorry, Heather. Sorry that I kissed you." The look of regret was plain on his face, and she didn't know if she was happy about that or not.

"Back when we were kids, back when we —well, *you know*. Right before you left town again after visiting Liv when Emily was first born. We agreed we'd just be friends. I know we did."

"So, why did you kiss me that time last year?"

"It was actually *two* years ago." He shook his

head. "You've been mad at me for two years, Heather."

Actually, she'd been mad at him for sixteen years, ever since that trip to town when Emily was born. But he didn't even realize that, because she had rarely come back to town, and when she did it was just to see Liv and Emily for a quick visit. She'd learned to avoid him when she was in town. Who knew that all the avoiding of her father for so many years would turn into such a helpful skill she could use with Jesse.

"You slapped me when I kissed you. I was... surprised."

"Well, you surprised *me*." And surprised her how much she'd enjoyed the kiss. You know, before she'd decided to slap him.

"I know I did. I surprised *myself*. But then after you slapped me, you said I'd ruined things between us and ran off. I should have chased after you and we could have sorted it out."

"I know. It was... silly of me. I shouldn't have run off."

"But that's what you do." His tone was more stating a fact than accusing her.

"But then... when I did come to talk to you..."

"Right, I had Shelly over. And it was

awkward. I was actually telling Shelly that I didn't think things were working out between us. Between Shelly and I."

"Yet, you're still seeing her, I hear." And it shouldn't bother her... it *didn't* bother her. It didn't.

"We're just friends."

"I see." She wondered if Shelly knew that...

"Anyway, tonight was fun, wasn't it? Hanging out with Liv and Austin? And not being mad at each other?" He paused and looked directly at her. "I'd like to get back to being friends. I've missed you. Do you think we could try that? Being friends?"

She just didn't know what to say to him. She knew what he wanted to hear. That they could be friends. That things could go back to how they were sixteen years ago.

But things were just so complicated. It was almost easier to be mad at him and avoid him. Being friends would be... difficult.

He sat there staring, waiting.

She let out a long sigh. "We could try. But I don't think things can ever be like they were before." Too much time had passed. Too many hurt feelings. Too many secrets and lies...

A brief look of sadness clouded his eyes.

"Maybe not. But I'd sure like to try. I miss the Heather you used to be."

"That Heather is long gone, Jesse. She doesn't exist anymore. People change."

"If the new Heather could at least not run away every time she sees me, I'd be fine with starting there. Will that work?" His easy smile urged her to say yes.

She gave in and finally smiled back at him. It was a weak smile, but it was the best she could do. Besides, if she said yes, then maybe this whole conversation could end. "Yes, the new Heather could try and not run the other direction when she sees you."

"That's at least a start." He stood and reached out a hand. "Come on, I'll walk you the rest of the way home."

Heather sat outside on her balcony long after Jesse had walked her to the lobby doors of her building. She hadn't even considered asking him up to her condo. Okay, maybe she had for a brief moment before common sense kicked in. She needed time to process the evening.

She admitted she had fun at dinner... in a

stressful kind of way. The easy conversation and laughter had helped to ease her stress by the end of the meal. At least somewhat. By the end of the dinner, she'd even imagined that she could have a slightly uneasy *acquaintance* relationship with Jesse. Acquaintance. That was a good word. That would work. Maybe.

But then he'd offered—more like insisted—that he walk her home. And then insisted they talk. He wanted to be friends again. And any way she looked at it, she just wasn't sure that would work.

So much time had passed. She'd gotten used to not having him in her life. When she was being extremely honest with herself—which, granted, was not often—she could admit how much she missed him. He always seemed to get her. Understand her. Know what she was feeling, sometimes more than she'd admit to herself.

But was she ready to get close to him again? And if she did, and he still had that connection to her... would he figure out things that she really, *really* didn't want him to know?

CHAPTER 5

E velyn paged through her recipe binder, jotting down ideas for some items Jesse could serve on The Destiny. He'd asked her to come up with some menus and help the cook by working a few evenings on the boat. She had to convert some recipes into larger quantities, but she was getting quite handy at that after working here at the cafe.

She looked up when Livy and Donna came into the kitchen.

"Hey, Evie, we want to talk to you," Donna said.

"Sure, what about? Are you two okay with me helping Jesse?" She should have asked them to make sure. She'd have to take a few nights off to help him, and she didn't want to bring any competition to the cafe.

"Oh, we're fine with that," Livy assured her.

"Okay, what's up?" She put down her pen.

"So, we've come to a decision. A family decision," Donna said as she took a seat at the counter beside Evelyn. "We want you to have part ownership in the cafe."

"What?" Had she heard that correctly? An *owner?* "But I didn't invest in it."

"Technically, I didn't either very much," Livy said as she leaned against the counter. "Heather put up most of the money. I just invested my time in the business plan and putting the cafe together."

Donna leaned forward and tapped the counter. "You work very hard here. And Parker's —the store and the cafe—are both family businesses. There's no reason for you not to have a split of the profits."

"Besides, your cooking is the reason that the cafe is so successful," Livy insisted.

"You're sure?" Evelyn tried to process all this. She'd have part of the profits? Something she'd helped create. Pride soared through her. Who would have thought on that day she found out Darren was divorcing her and leaving her with nothing, that she'd get to this point in her life, and so soon?

"We're positive." Livy jumped up and hugged her. "Parker women stick together. And if you want to be part of Parker business, then you deserve this."

"I'm so surprised. I've never really worked at Parker's until the cafe. Well, except a bit as a young girl to help out Grandmother."

"You're a part of Parker's now. And I'm going to pour us all some coffee to celebrate." Donna got up and grabbed the drinks. She handed them each a mug and raised hers. "To the Parker women."

Evelyn fought back tears. She was so lucky to have such a great family. And she was very proud that she could now support herself. After all those years of Darren insisting she not get a job. That she had to be available at a moment's notice to throw a dinner party for him or run his errands. Look how far she'd come. She raised her mug as a wide grin spread across her face. "To the Parker women."

CHAPTER 6

Donna walked into The Cabot Hotel to meet Barry for dinner. She'd managed to run home and change into some nice slacks and a top, thanks to a shopping spree with Olivia and Heather earlier this year. Olivia kept making noises that they should go shopping again. Donna wasn't really opposed to that suggestion now that she was seeing Barry all the time.

She told the hostess that she was meeting Barry, and the woman smiled and nodded. "Right this way."

The woman led her through the dining room, and she frowned when she didn't see Barry anywhere. Maybe she'd gotten here before him? The hostess continued to the far end of the room and paused by a doorway. "He's waiting for you in here."

Donna stepped through the doorway and Barry walked up to her. He was so handsome that it sometimes took her breath away. And this was one of those times. His smile. His just for her smile. It made her weak in the knees, and she was much too old for that nonsense. Yet... her heart fluttered at that smile. He kissed her cheek and stood back.

She peered into the room. "Oh, my." The small room held a single table that was set for two with a fancy tablecloth. Candles flickered gently next to a beautiful arrangement of flowers adorning the center of the table. A large window looked out over the bay. "I didn't even know this room existed."

"It actually just recently got finished. I managed to snag it for our dinner tonight." He led her over to the table.

"It's lovely." She sat down in the chair Barry held out for her.

He sat down across the table. "I ordered some champagne. I hope that's okay."

"That sounds wonderful. What's the occasion?"

"I just wanted to have a special evening with my favorite gal." He grinned and handed her a glass of champagne.

They sipped their champagne for a bit and chatted about their days. She loved this. Just spending time with him. They saw each other almost every evening now unless one of them got tied up with work. He was so easy to talk to, and she enjoyed hearing all the little details of his day.

Once they'd ordered their meals, Barry stood. "Let's go look out at the view." He took her hand and they walked over to the window.

"It's so beautiful out there. The sun is almost ready to set, and the sky is so glorious with all those colors."

He smiled. "I know you love your sunsets."

She laughed. "I do."

He took her hand, and she immediately felt its warmth. A warmth that spread through her. "So... Donna. We've been dating for a while now, and I really, really enjoy spending time with you. I care about you. I love you."

"I love you, too." Somehow that had become easier for her to say. Something she never would have believed the first time she said it to him after deliberating for so long on whether she did actually love him and whether she could tell him.

He squeezed her hand. "I was wondering... I mean..."

Barry looked nervous, and he *never* looked nervous. He was always confident and self-assured. Her forehead crinkled as she watched him.

He suddenly grasped her other hand and held both of them in his. "Donna. I love you. I know you hate change."

She did hate change... She eyed him with a bit of suspicion. What did he want to change? Things were great just like they were right now.

"But I do want things to... change. I want to spend the rest of my life with you. I—" He paused and look right at her, deep into her eyes, maybe into her very soul. "Will you marry me?"

Somehow a delicate ring box appeared with a perfect single diamond in a beautiful yet simple setting.

She stood silently as shock bolted through her.

She hadn't been expecting this. Not at all.

He stood patiently waiting for an answer. She looked at the ring, back up to his face, back down at the ring.

Then she finally looked back up into those eyes of his. Got lost in them. Her heart pounded in her chest, and she reached out to touch his arm. "Yes. I'd very much like to marry you."

A wide, delighted grin spread across his face. "Now that's the answer I was hoping for." He took the ring out of the box and slipped it on her finger.

She stared down at her hand and slowly moved it back and forth, letting the light hit the stone. "I love this ring."

"I'm glad." He pulled her into his arms and kissed her. "You made me the happiest man in Moonbeam."

She leaned against him, letting it all sink in.

She had just gotten engaged.

She was going to marry Barry.

Happiness swept through her. This was one change that she was actually looking forward to.

Donna and Barry enjoyed a nice dinner of *something...* she wasn't really sure. She knew they had ordered. And she'd eaten. But everything seemed like a blur right now. They finished the meal by splitting a piece of delicious chocolate cake. Now *that* she remembered.

A knock sounded at the door to their private room. "Come in," Barry called out.

Delbert stood in the door with a grin on his face. "Okay, I asked your server if Donna was wearing the ring. So I assume she said yes?"

"You knew about this?" She asked.

"Yes, Delbert helped me plan all of this and make it all special."

"It was special." She smiled at Del. "And yes, I said yes."

"I'm very happy for both of you. Couldn't happen to nicer people. So have you set a date yet?"

"I... no... we haven't really talked about it," she said. Oh, there was going to be so much planning to do.

"The sooner the better as far as I'm concerned." Barry's mouth spread into a coaxing grin. "Right?"

"It takes time to plan a wedding. And we'll have to find a venue. They book out quickly here in Moonbeam." And where *did* she want the wedding?

"You could have it here at The Cabot. In

the ballroom," Delbert offered. "I'd love to host the wedding for you."

"Oh, that's kind... but I'm hoping for a smaller wedding, I think." She turned to Barry. "Is that okay? Smaller?"

"I'm happy with whatever you want. Anything. But I'll add again, the sooner the better."

"We've almost finished renovating the covered pavilion beside the hotel. You've seen it, right? It looks out over the harbor. It will hold up to 120 guests or so. We're hoping it will be popular as a rental space. You could kick off our events. We don't have any reservations for the pavilion yet. The view from there is fabulous, and with it being covered, you can have an outside wedding without worry about a rain shower popping up."

"That might work." She nodded. She liked that idea. Outside without worry about the unpredictable pop-up storms that often plagued the area. Looking out over her beloved bay. It sounded perfect.

"So how soon?" Barry's eyes twinkled with excitement.

She laughed. "I don't know. I need some

time to plan. How about in three to four months?"

"One," he countered emphatically.

She looked over at him with his eager expression, and she couldn't find one reason to delay. She was just as eager to marry him and start their life together. "The Harbor Festival is in a few weeks. That's going to keep us busy. But then...after that? How about six weeks?"

"I'll take it." Barry got up, came around to her side of the table, and pulled her to her feet, wrapping his arms around her. "I'm one lucky guy, Delbert."

"You are." Delbert nodded. "I'll leave you two alone. And congrats."

She looked up into Barry's eyes. "Six weeks. That's not much time."

"I'd marry you tomorrow if you'd say yes to it." His eyes shone with happiness.

She could do this. Pull off a wedding—she was getting *married*—in six weeks. She could. Evelyn would help. And so would Olivia. The diamond sparkled on her hand and caught her attention again. She sure had a lot to tell the Parker women.

Tomorrow. She'd tell them tomorrow.

Tonight it was just Barry and her and a magical evening together.

CHAPTER 7

Donna walked into the kitchen of the cafe the next morning after the breakfast rush had died down. Evelyn and Olivia were sitting at a table sorting through invoices.

Evelyn looked up and smiled. "Morning, Donna. Grab a cup of coffee and join us."

She walked over, grabbed a mug, and returned with her coffee, settling into a chair across from Evelyn and Olivia. She carefully kept her left hand tucked under the table.

Olivia looked over at her and frowned. "You okay, Mom?"

"Yes, I'm fine."

"You look a bit flushed."

"I do?" She automatically reached up to push her hair away from her face.

... with her left hand.

"Mom!" Olivia jumped up and raced around the table and grabbed her hand. "What is this?"

"Donna?" Evelyn's eyes widened.

"This is what I was coming to tell you two. Barry asked me to marry him."

"And you said yes!" Olivia threw her arms around her and hugged her tightly. "I'm so happy for you."

Evelyn got up and came around and took her hand, looking at the ring. "It's beautiful, Donna. Just lovely. And I'm very happy for you two."

"Thanks." She sat with a silly grin resting on her face as Olivia and Evelyn slipped back into their chairs.

"Tell me everything. When? Where?" Olivia leaned forward.

"We went to dinner at The Cabot. He reserved a private dining room. He asked me there. It was all so very romantic." Terribly romantic. Every detail was still etched clearly in her mind.

"And when are you planning on getting married?"

Donna gave them a rueful grin. "Um... in six weeks?"

"Really?" Olivia's mouth fell open.

"At the pavilion at The Cabot."

"Oh, Mom. That will be a lovely place to get married." Olivia jumped up and grabbed a pad of paper. "Okay. You know me. The ultimate list maker. Let's start a list of everything that needs to be done."

"A dress, invitations, flowers, a caterer..." Evelyn started counting on her fingers.

"Evie, do you think you could do the food? I mean, and be *in* my wedding?" Suddenly the enormity of all she was asking her family to do in such a short time swept over her.

"Oh, yes. I can make it work. Melody Tanner will help us. This is great."

She turned to Olivia. "And you'll be in my wedding, too?"

"Of course, Mom."

"I just want a small wedding. Family and a few close friends. I was thinking of making it kind of vintage-y. Especially since it's at The Cabot."

"I can help you plan everything," Evelyn insisted. "Oh, I can already think of ideas for the centerpieces on the table and decorations to make it feel like a vintage wedding."

"Take her up on that, Mom. You know Aunt Evelyn is the best event planner in Moonbeam. Probably in the whole state."

"I'll take all the help I can get."

"When do you want to go dress shopping?" Olivia asked. "You don't have much time."

"I was actually thinking of wearing Grace Parker's wedding dress. We still have it carefully sealed up and packed away. It was so beautiful and simple. I just think I'd love to feel like... like the history of our family was there with me at the wedding."

"That's a lovely idea." Evelyn nodded. "We'll drag it out of storage and you can try it on. I've heard of this wonderful seamstress on Belle Island. Her name is Ruby. If it needs to be altered, we'll contact her."

"And you two could pick out whatever dresses you'd like." Because they both were better at choosing clothes than she'd ever be. She trusted their judgement.

"We'll find something simple that fits in with your vintage feel, won't we, Evelyn?" Olivia's eyes lit up.

"Yes, we'll go shopping as soon as possible."

Evelyn smiled. "Donna, I'm just so very happy for you. You deserve this happiness and Barry is a great guy."

"Thanks, Evie. I should get back to work. But I wanted you two to be the first to know." Elation still clung to her, warring with her desire to plan everything and her responsibility to her job. How was she ever going to balance everything in the next few weeks?

"First to know what?" Heather walked into the kitchen.

"Mom, show her."

Donna held up her hand self-consciously.

"Whoop." Heather rushed over and hugged her. "Aunt Donna, that is great. Fabulous."

"And her wedding is in six weeks at the pavilion at The Cabot."

"It looks like we Parker women have a lot of planning to do." Heather grinned and hugged her again. "Gosh, a wedding. That's just fabulous."

"Come on, I'll pour us all another cup of coffee and we'll make more plans." Evelyn got up to grab the coffee.

Maybe work could wait for just a bit. It only made sense to get as much planning done as possible as soon as possible. She convinced herself that was the right decision as they sat for more than an hour making lists of guests and planning food and flowers. And laughing. Lots of laughing.

She looked around at the faces of the Parker women. A feeling of incredible rightness and luck flowed through her. There was nothing in the world like being part of this incredible family.

Though there was still one minor hurdle she had to pass...

She—or *someone*—still needed to tell her mother the news.

CHAPTER 8

Olivia and Austin met at The Destiny on Monday evening as planned and waited at the end of the pier for Heather. "Do you think we did the right thing? You know, with conspiring for you and Jesse to just happen to show up at Jimmy's?"

"Neither Jesse nor Heather thought it was a coincidence." Austin laughed. "But I think they eventually had a good time."

"And he walked Heather home, there is that. And they agreed, albeit grudgingly, to come on The Destiny tonight." She looked down the pier. "Sh, here comes Heather."

Heather looked a bit wary, but beautiful, as she approached. She wore a simple yellow dress and teal flats, with her hair swept back in a clip. "I made it," she said.

"You did." Olivia hugged her. "We waited to board with you." More to the truth, she was afraid if they didn't wait here, Heather might chicken out.

"Let's go aboard." Austin led the way to the gangplank.

"Wow, look at this." Olivia looked around in surprise as they entered the boat. "Jesse has really fixed this up nice."

"It... it is nice," Heather said as if she was surprised herself.

Jesse waved from the distance and motioned for them to head upstairs to the open deck. They grabbed drinks at the bar and climbed up the spiral stairs to the top deck. They stood by the railing, and soon the boat cast off and they headed into the harbor.

"Oh, look. Dolphins," Heather pointed out beside the boat.

Olivia shaded her eyes and caught sight of a pair of dolphins arcing out of the water before splashing back down.

They watched as the boat slipped away from Moonbeam, sliced through the waters of the bay, and headed for the coast.

"Hey," Jesse said as he walked up to them. "Beautiful night."

"It is," Olivia agreed. "And Jesse, you've really done your magic on the boat. She's wonderful."

"Thanks."

"It really is nice," Heather added. "You've done a great job refurbishing her.

Jesse's eyes lit up at Heather's compliment.

But then Heather and Jesse stood silent. She wanted to roll her eyes at them. Or shake them. Or something. She'd have to try to break the ice herself. "So, you've got another skipper, I take it?"

"Yes, I actually have two other qualified captains now, so it's not always just me. Plus a few deckhands, and then the cook and servers." Jesse's eye shone with pride. "It took a while to get to this point, but I'm pleased."

"And now that your friend got your website updated and running, I bet that helps, too," Austin teased.

"I do appreciate all you did on that, buddy. I do."

"Austin is like magic when it comes to all things internet and online," Olivia said, smiling at Austin and tucking her hand in the crook of his arm.

Then silence again. She wished someone else would pick up the slack tonight. She eyed Austin.

He nodded in response and turned toward Heather. "So, do you have a website for your art?"

"I do. It's fairly simple. I think it loads slowly though, with all the photos of my work. And I really need to get an updated list where my work can be found. But my web person is so hard to get ahold of for updates."

"I could help you update it and make it so you could do all your future updates yourself," Austin offered.

"You could do that?"

"I could."

"I'd love that. I hate to be dependent on anyone for... well, anything." Heather shrugged.

Jesse had to keep himself from laughing out loud at Heather's understatement. No, she didn't like to depend on anyone but herself. Ever. For anything. Never had.

Austin and Heather chatted a bit about her website and he watched her from the corner of his eyes. She loved her career, that much was evident. He was happy she'd found such success with her work. Her work seemed to hit the emotional spot that made people connect to it. From her heartwarming scenes to her quirkier, humorous work on some greeting cards he'd spotted at the card shop. He'd secretly bought a couple of cards and put them in his desk. Not to send to anyone, just to help him still feel connected to Heather.

He rarely admitted to himself how much he missed her. Sometimes he wished they were back when they were kids and could have a do-over. Maybe she'd never have moved away.

Or something.

But life didn't give a person do-overs. You lived with the consequences of the choices you made.

"Jesse?"

Livy's voice brought him back to the present. "What?"

"I was asking if you could join us for dinner, or if you're going to be too busy with the boat."

"If you don't mind waiting a bit, I can join you. Just let me go check on a few things."

"We'll wait," Heather said.

And that surprised him. He hurried off to check with the second mate, popped into the galley to see if the cook needed anything, then met Heather, Livy, and Austin down by the buffet line. They all grabbed some food and headed to a table by the large windows on the boat.

"This is really great food, Jesse," Livy complimented him.

"And I expect it to get better with Heather's mom's help."

"Nothing like some healthy competition for the dining business in town," Livy joked.

"I didn't mean to take over anything from the cafe," he was quick to assure her.

"I'm pretty sure there's room for both of us in Moonbeam. You're more a leisurely, spend-an-evening place. We're come in and get a good home-cooked meal."

Jesse was relieved. The last thing he wanted was any trouble in his life, especially since things were maybe... sort of... kind of... starting to get better between him and Heather.

They ate their meal and chatted about

Parker's Cafe and the upcoming Harbor Festival at the town park on the harbor.

"We're going to have a booth with food from Sea Glass Cafe at the festival," Livy said.

"I'll be busy running hourly boat tours. Then that evening we stay docked but open up our buffet. We've already got a lot of reservations for dinner. We're going to put extra tables on the top deck," Jesse said.

"Hey, Heather. You should do a booth with some of your prints," Livy said. "I bet the townsfolk would love to be able to buy some of them. You know, local girl makes it good."

"I thought I'd just help out at the cafe's booth, or back at the cafe." Heather frowned. "And I'm not sure with a few stores in town carrying my work that it would be a good idea to have a booth. I'd like to participate in some way, though."

"I think the booth is a good idea. You should think about it," Livy insisted.

"Or, you know... they are doing that fundraiser for the library. Maybe you could put up a few of your originals for auction. I bet they'd bring in a lot of money." Jesse paused for a second, unsure if he was being too forward or insistent. "You know, if you wanted to." He had no idea if she'd want to auction her original work.

Heather's eyes lit up. "That's a great idea. I could do that. I even have the original illustration I did of the harbor walk and the gazebo by the town park."

"That's a great idea," Livy agreed. "People love your work."

"Thanks." Heather shifted uncomfortably in her seat at the praise.

"Your work is really great, Heather."

She blushed a deep pink—which looked adorable on her.

"Enough about my work." She tried to look nonchalant and concentrated on taking a sip of her drink.

"I should go check on things, again. I'll meet you upstairs in a bit?" Jesse rose.

"Sure, we'll see you up top," Austin said.

Jesse hurried off to check things, eager to rush back and enjoy more of the evening. But a bit of a crisis in the kitchen, a lost case of wine, and the wind picking up so that he was needed to tie up the boat when it docked kept him away from his guests.

After they docked and the rest of the guests had disembarked, he met his three friends back in the main room of the ship. Friends. Surely he was getting back to being Heather's friend now, wasn't he?

Heather admitted she'd had a really nice time tonight on The Destiny. At least once she'd let herself relax. The friendly banter had been nice, and it was always fun to spend time with Livy. There hadn't been a lot of that the last few months except while they worked at the cafe.

Then there was Jesse. Standing here in the main room of The Destiny looking impossibly handsome. He'd done such a good job with refurbishing the boat, and it was clear that he was proud of it. She could almost—*almost* —imagine being friends with him again.

"I'm going to walk Livy home," Austin said. "Jesse, you going to escort Heather home?"

"I don't—" Heather started to speak.

"Yes, I plan on it." Jesse paused and looked at her. "If that's okay?"

She nodded. She certainly didn't need the escort, but she realized she'd *welcome* his company. Now that was a change that startled her.

Austin and Livy left, and she hung out while Jesse made sure everything was locked up for the night on the boat. Then they headed down the gangplank.

"I had a good time on your boat. It's really nice."

"Thanks, I really loved having all of you aboard."

They headed down the pier at the marina and walked by the entrance to the wharf. As they passed a crowd, she heard one of the Jenkins twins call out. "Yoo-hoo! Heather! Jesse!"

They turned to see the women headed toward them. "Oh, boy," Heather whispered but put on a smile.

"Oh, Heather. How good to see you. And Jesse. Both of you. Together." The twin raised her eyebrow and smiled knowingly.

"It's been so long since Jackie and I have seen you together." So it must be Jillian talking. Good. Now she had them sorted out.

"I don't know what caused the rift between you two, but it is good to see that you've patched things up."

Heather stared at them. Even the twins knew that she and Jesse had been on the outs?

She had thought it was only she and Jesse who knew that. And possibly Livy.

"We were just out on The Destiny," Jesse offered.

Did he not know that was just going to fuel gossip? She looked at him quickly and raised an eyebrow. He semi-shrugged.

"We must go on The Destiny soon," Jillian said.

"We must." Jackie nodded.

"Anytime, ladies. Be glad to have you." Jesse smiled at them.

"It was great to see you, but Jesse, I really should be going." Heather tried to pull him away from the ladies.

"Good to see you too, dear." Jillian gave her a wide smile. "I hope to see both of you—*together*—soon.

She grabbed Jesse's arm and pulled him away from the wharf and onto the harbor walk. "Are you crazy? Why give them anything to talk about?"

"They're harmless." He shrugged.

"But people will be talking about us now."

"Maybe. Until something new comes along to talk about. Besides, I don't care if people know that you came on The Destiny."

She didn't know how she felt about that. Even just a tentative friendship with Jesse was all new to her.

They walked side by side in the moonlight and the soft sea breeze. His hand brushed hers briefly, and she ignored it as she concentrated on the intricate boardwalk design stamped into the cement of the harbor walk. The old plank walkway had long since been replaced with this concrete one, but the designers had done their best to mimic the old wooden one. Why she was thinking about the actual harbor walkway just then was beyond her. But she was. Like the many benches scattered along the walk. The lampposts spread along the walk and the view of a handful of boats moored out in the harbor, some dark, and some with dim lights on. She wondered if people were spending the night on the boats all moored out there.

"What are you thinking about? I can see you're thinking." Jesse interrupted her thoughts.

She laughed and pointed out to the bay. "Those boats moored out there. Do people stay on them out there?"

"A few people do. Sometimes. It's pretty peaceful sleeping out there with the gentle rocking of the boat. I'm actually thinking of buying a used trawler boat I found. It needs some work, but it would be fun to have a boat to putter around in... that isn't as big as The Destiny. A personal boat."

"Really? You'd have time for that?"

He grinned. "Well, that's my biggest hold-up. I feel like I don't have much time now. If I got a boat to fix up—and let me tell you, there's enough to fix on The Destiny all the time—I don't know where I'd find the time."

"But you should try and find time to do things for yourself. Things you love to do."

"Well, I do love running The Destiny, there is that. It rarely feels like an actual job. I love going out on her day after day. It was such a dream of mine to own my own business, and now I do."

"I feel that way about my illustrations. They aren't work." She grinned. "And people pay me for my art. It's a great career."

They got to the lobby of her condo, and she considered asking him up. Before she could decide, he turned to her.

"So, would you like to go out to dinner with me?" he asked, then quickly added, "Just as friends, of course. I had a good time tonight. We used to meet for drinks or dinner all the time. You know, before... before things got messed up."

She pondered her answer. She wanted to say no. But she wanted to say yes. The two answers warred with each other.

"Yes, that sounds like fun." To her utter surprise, it appeared that yes won the battle.

His mouth spread into a wide grin. "Great. How about next Monday night? I don't have a dinner cruise that night. We're doing a big noontime rental cruise for a local church group. I should be finished up by late afternoon."

"Monday works."

"Where do you want to go?"

"I don't know."

"How about Magic Cafe over on Belle Island?" Jesse suggested.

"Oh, I haven't been there in years. That sounds like fun. I love that place."

"I'll swing by and pick you up about six? If we time it right, we'll get to see one of the island's famous sunsets."

"That sounds great."

"I better run. It's getting late." He gave her a small smile and turned to leave.

"Night, Jesse."

He turned back to her. "Night, Heather.

Had a great time." And with that, he disappeared down the sidewalk.

If she didn't know better, she'd just said yes to a date with Jesse Brown. Something she thought would never, ever happen.

CHAPTER 9

The next afternoon, Heather found Livy up in the storage room over the cafe, sorting through boxes. "Hey, cuz."

"Hey, Heather, what's up?"

"I came to help you clear out the room."

"I'm sure not going to say no to help." Livy flung her arms wide. "Over there is the pitch stack. You won't believe some of the junk I've found. Over there is stuff to actually move into storage and keep."

"I'm on it." Heather walked over and pried open a box. "Oh, look. An entire box of fliers from a sale back in 1952." She laughed. "I'm going to save a couple of them, but the rest can be recycled."

They methodically opened every last box,

laughing at the things that had been kept for years and years. Then they dragged the junk downstairs and out back and piled it high in the dumpster. A pile was made to haul to the recycling center and the other boxes were placed in storage.

"Look, there are some wooden shelves we could use for the displays." Livy pointed to a row of shelves on the back wall.

"Those would be perfect." Heather walked over to them. "Oh, look, they have Parker carved into them. Do you think these were made by Grace's husband when they opened the store?" She ran her fingers over the smooth wood and wiped away some dust. "Yes, look, he carved in the year, too. 1926. He did some very nice woodwork, did't he?"

"He did. He made that cradle I used for Emily when she was first born. Do you remember it?" Livy smiled. "It was nice having it after it had been used by so many generations of babies in our family. Lots of history with the cradle. A whole lot."

An unexpected twang of sadness crept over her. Would a child of hers ever be part of that history? She pushed the thought away. It was silly to dwell on that now.

They headed back to the now cleared out room. Livy sank onto the floor. "I'm exhausted."

"Me, too." Heather sat beside her and leaned against the brick wall. "I see potential in this space, though."

"I do, too. I've already ordered some beachy Christmas things. Cards, signs, mugs. And we'll sell Parker's General Store and Sea Glass Cafe mugs, too. Some general Moonbeam things like t-shirts and souvenirs. I think I'll do a spring section and a summer section. Then we'll filter the holiday things into the appropriate season."

"Once the merchandise comes in, I'll help you set it up."

"That would be great. I'm going to pick a grand opening day for it. I'll have Emily post on the website and social media. Kind of play it up. Generate some buzz." She laughed. "Generate buzz. That's what Emily says. Who knew we needed buzz? Anyway, hopefully we'll generate some traffic and let people know about it."

"Oh, and I can paint you a sign to put at the bottom of the stairs saying the seasonal room is up here."

"Perfect." Livy looked over at her and frowned. "So, I know you said you came over today to help... but what else? You have that look on your face."

"What look?"

"The one that says you have something to tell me." Livy wrapped her arms around her knees and rested her chin on her arms. "So, you might as well tell me. You know I'll drag it out of you."

"I... well, it appears I have a date with Jesse." A wave of tentative eagerness washed through her, but she tried to hide it from her cousin. Not that it would ever happen. Livy could always tell when she was hiding something. Well, usually she could.

Livy sat up straight and grinned. "You do? That's awesome. Great. Fantastic."

"Tell me how you really feel." She grinned back at her cousin. That's one thing about Livy, she never held back on her enthusiasm.

"Where, when? Give me the details."

"On Monday. We're going over to Belle Island to Magic Cafe."

"I haven't been there in a long time," Livy said. "That's a great choice. Beautiful view and away from the town's prying eyes here in Moonbeam.

"Exactly."

Livy raised her eyebrows and leaned forward. "So, I guess you guys have worked things out?"

"Pretty much." Not everything. Some things just couldn't be worked out. But at least they were friends again. Or friendly. Or something. Maybe she'd figure it out on their date.

Maybe.

CHAPTER 10

The Parker women all gathered at Donna's on Sunday for brunch in celebration of her news. Evelyn made a delicious egg casserole along with her famous cinnamon rolls. Heather brought a fruit tray, and Olivia showed up with the makings for mimosas.

Donna enjoyed their little celebration. She wasn't used to being the center of attention, but she was having fun. They sat around after brunch, sipping drinks and chatting. Emily enthusiastically regaled them with all the photos she'd added to the website and her plans for hyping the new seasonal room. It was just a perfect family day.

Evelyn dug out a pad of paper and jotted down more things for the wedding to-do list.

Donna couldn't believe how much they'd already accomplished on the wedding in just a few short days. Evelyn put down her pen and raised her glass. "To the wonderful wedding Donna is going to have."

Olivia laughed. "We sure toast a lot in this family."

"That we do," Donna agreed.

They raised their mimosa glasses, and Emily raised her glass of orange juice, and they clinked glasses.

"Girls? Are you here?"

Donna stiffened at the sound of her mother's voice.

They all stopped, frozen in place for a moment before they hastily put down their glasses.

Patricia swept into the kitchen. "There you are."

"Mother, what are you doing here? If we'd known you were coming to town, we would have invited you to our little celebration," Evelyn said.

Donna gave her sister a hard look, hoping their mother didn't catch on to the *celebration* word. She hadn't actually told her the news yet.

But Patricia Beale missed nothing. "What celebration?"

Donna rose and walked over to her mother. "I was going to call and tell you. Today. I was going to call today." She held out her hand. "Barry asked me to marry him."

Patricia stood silent for a long moment, looking at the ring. "I see. Are you certain that's what you want to do?"

"I'm sure, Mom."

"You've been on your own for a long time. And men can be... difficult. And aren't you a bit old for planning a wedding?"

Ouch. Her mother could be... blunt. "Mom, I love him."

"That's fine, but it doesn't mean you have to marry him." Patricia shook her head.

Evelyn jumped up. "She wants to marry him. And he's a great guy. Really great."

Olivia came to stand beside her. "Grandmother, he makes Mom happy. We're all thrilled for her. And we all adore Barry."

Emily and Heather came to stand beside her, too. All the Parker women, defending her. Though, *technically*, the town thought of Patricia as a Parker woman, too.

"They're going to get married in six weeks. At the pavilion at The Cabot," Heather added.

Patricia's eyes clouded for a moment and a slight frown crossed her face. "The Cabot? Really?"

"Yes, Delbert offered the pavilion," Donna explained. "I think it will be lovely. We've already done a lot of the planning."

"But exactly six weeks from this weekend?" Patricia's frown deepened.

"Yes."

"You can't get married that weekend." Her mother shook her head.

"Why not?"

"Because that's when I've planned to move to Sunrise Village. There are six of us moving from our retirement place in Naples to the new one opening here. I'll need you girls to help."

"Grandmother, I'm pretty sure a wedding tops a move. You can change your move-in date," Olivia insisted.

"I don't want to change it. All my friends are moving in then." Patricia looked appalled that Olivia had even suggested it.

Donna wavered. It was sometimes easier not to challenge her mother. But they'd already made plans. Even picked out flowers and booked a photographer for that date.

"We can help you the next week after Mom gets married," Olivia insisted.

"If invitations haven't been sent, Donna should move her date." Patricia's eyes flashed, determined in her stance. Determined to win the argument.

Evelyn looked at Donna, shook her head, and stepped forward. "Donna is *not* changing her wedding day because you're moving. We're happy to have you back here in Moonbeam, but... I won't let Donna change her day." Evie turned to look at her. "I know that's what you're thinking. It's easier to change than to stand up to Mother." Her sister turned back to their mom. "But, Mother, the wedding isn't changing."

"Well... I... never," Patricia sputtered. "I don't see why *I* need to change my plans."

"You don't have to, if you don't want to. But then you'll miss the wedding," Emily said. "You don't want to do that, do you?"

"I... I supposed if there's no getting around it. I'll change my movers. Maybe they can come a few days before that."

"That's fine, but we'll be busy with Donna's

wedding that week, so we won't have time to help you very much." Evelyn stood tall, facing their mother.

"Fine. I'll do it all on my own." Patricia whirled around and headed for the door, her heels clicking precisely on the tile floor, dismissing her daughters with every step.

"We'll be glad to help with anything you need after the wedding," Heather called out.

Patricia ignored all of them and slammed the door behind her as she left.

Donna and Evelyn crossed over and peeked out the front window. "She's still using a driver. I wonder why she was in town today. She never said." Donna sighed as they headed back to the kitchen.

"Well, that was... pleasant." Olivia stood by Heather, mimosas in hand.

"What she meant to say was congratulations, Donna. I'm so happy for you." Heather rolled her eyes.

Donna grabbed her drink and turned to Evelyn. "I don't know what's happened to you in the last few months, but that was impressive. Standing up to Mother like that."

Evelyn's smile was laced with confidence. "I thought so, too. I'm just tired of people trying to push me around. Or push you. Or anyone for that matter."

"And she's right, Grams. Weddings are more important than a moving date. The move can be... well, moved." Emily slipped into her chair.

"I still feel a bit guilty for not moving my date. She's so upset." Donna knew her mother was being unreasonable, but still, years of giving into the woman's demands was a habit that was hard to break.

Evelyn threaded her arm around her. "She's upset because she didn't get her way. It's going to be fine. Mom will get over it."

"You think she'll even come to the wedding?" Donna wasn't sure.

"Of course," Evie insisted. But her voice didn't sound very convincing.

CHAPTER 11

On Monday, Heather put on a simple white sundress with delicate yellow flowers on it for her date with Jesse. She had to admit that half her wardrobe seemed to be made up of yellow. Probably because it was her favorite color. It was cheerful, bright—hopeful even. Yellow even managed to find its way into much of her artwork.

She took one last look in the mirror. A touch of makeup and her hair pulled back in a French braid. She knew Jesse had always liked her hair down, but it was warm this evening and they were going to be sitting outside at Magic Cafe.

She'd never really dated Jesse. They'd just hung out as friends. Hung out a lot. And even though this kind of felt like a date, was it really?

Did he think of this as just hanging out like they used to?

Too much thinking.

She grabbed a small clutch bag, threw her keys and cell phone in it, and went to wait for Jesse.

She paced back and forth in the living room. Twelve steps this way. Twelve steps back. This was silly. She might as well go downstairs and wait for him in the lobby. She could just as easily pace down there.

As she waited for the elevator, she stared at her reflection in the shiny doors, trying not to pace. The door slid open and Jesse stood there with a wide grin spreading across his face when he saw her. A grin that said he was truly happy to see her. The kind of grin she used to get from him all those years ago when they were kids. When their lives weren't so complicated. And for a moment, she could almost imagine that they could go back to that.

"You look beautiful," Jesse said, giving her an admiring look.

The warmth of a blush crept across her cheeks. "You clean up pretty nice yourself." Actually, he looked incredibly handsome in slacks and a collared knit shirt stretched tight across his broad chest. He had that tanned face so common to the locals who worked outside, and his blue eyes sparkled. So nice to not see them steely blue and annoyed with her.

They headed back down to the lobby and got into Jesse's car, a sensible silver sedan. But that would be Jesse. He was always sensible.

They drove across the bridge over Moonbeam Bay, then headed to Belle Island. The scenery of the familiar route slipped by as they rode in silence. An easy silence, though, so that was okay.

He pulled into the crushed shell parking lot, jumped out, and came around to open her door. She slid out and bumped into him slightly from the shifting shells beneath her shoes.

"Careful." He steadied her.

They headed into Magic Cafe, his hand on her elbow. She wasn't sure if that was to help her steady herself on the uneven surface or if he was afraid she'd change her mind and turn and run away.

"Well, look who's here." Tally, who owned Magic Cafe, gave them both a hug. "Haven't seen you two in a month of Sundays."

"It has been a while." Heather smiled at Tally's warm greeting.

"I see your work in quite a few of the shops here, Heather. And Jesse, I must get over and take a cruise on The Destiny. I hear great things about it."

"Any time. I'd love to have you," he said.

Tally led them to a table at the edge of the deck with an unobstructed view of the gulf. "Enjoy your meal. I'll pop back later when I can and we'll chat."

Heather looked over the menu. Not much had changed. She already knew she wanted grouper and hushpuppies. Her favorite here.

They ordered their meals and sat watching a few people sitting out on the beach, waiting for sunset. She wished she'd brought her iPad to do a quick sketch of the scene. But that would probably be rude.

Jesse laughed a knowing laugh. "You're wishing you could sketch this, aren't you?"

She looked up, knowing she'd been caught. "I was thinking that."

"I could ask Tally for some paper and a pen."

"No, but I do think I'll snap a quick photo if you don't mind." She took out her phone and took a few photos of people on the beach and then, before she could think of what she was doing, she snapped a photo of Jesse.

He winked at her with a devilish grin. "Hope you got my good side."

Self-conscious, she slipped the phone back in her purse. She was saved from further embarrassment by the arrival of their drinks. Tally carried her favorite local beer, too, and they'd both ordered it.

She leaned back in her chair, trying to relax. It used to just be so easy to be with Jesse, and she longed for it to be that way again.

Jesse watched as Heather put the bottle of beer up to her lips and took a sip of the icy beverage. No airs with this woman. She liked a good cold beer out of the bottle. A simple meal at a casual place like Jimmy's or Magic Cafe. He'd always liked that about her. She enjoyed the simple, ordinary things in life more than the fancy things that so many people thought were important.

He set down his beer and stretched out his legs, surprised at how relaxing the evening had been so far. He hadn't been certain how it would work out... but so far, so good. "So, have the Parker women been busy planning Donna's wedding?"

"We have. I can't believe how much we've gotten organized already. Between the wedding and the Harbor Festival, we've got quite a few really busy weeks."

"I suspect with Evelyn in charge of things, you won't have a thing to worry about. She's great at that sort of stuff."

"She is. My mother has a talent for making it look simple, too. Even though I know it's not. But she already had Donna pick out flowers, and she's ordered the invitations, too. They'll go out this week."

It briefly crossed his mind if he'd be on the short list for a wedding invite... or if maybe, just maybe Heather would ask him to be her date. He smiled as she continued.

"She's coordinating with The Cabot on seating and where they'll serve the buffet. Donna wants a simple buffet dinner, nothing fancy. And we're going with kind of vintage-y decorations. I think it will be beautiful."

He loved the way her eyes lit up when she talked about the wedding. And how proud she was of her mother. There had been so many years when Heather and her mother had barely spoken. Now, look at them. They'd worked together on opening the cafe, and now they were working on Donna's wedding.

He debated asking the next question on his mind, not wanting to alter the relaxed look on her face. "So... and I'm not sure I should ask..."

"Go ahead." She cocked her head to the side and sent him a questioning look.

"Have you seen your father recently?"

Her eyes clouded, and there was a slight twitch at the edge of her jaw, the one she got when she was holding back her temper. "Not recently. I hear he's been throwing all sorts of parties at the house with his new young whatever she is. I also heard he has to hire someone to plan the events because his new *whatever* evidently doesn't plan as well as mother did for him." A pleased look flashed across her face at that small detail.

"So, here's the thing. His new young *whatever* called and asked to book The Destiny for a party your dad wants to have."

"Really?" Her eyes widened, then narrowed. "And what did you say?"

"I said I had to check the schedule and get

back with her." He watched her carefully, knowing her face would give him the truth even if her words didn't.

She sighed. "You should accept his booking. He has tons of money to throw around. You might as well get some of it."

"You sure?"

"I'm sure. And the people he invites might lead to more business for you, too, once they see what a great job you've done with the boat."

He was *fairly* certain she was telling him the truth and not just what he wanted to hear. "You know I'll turn it down if it bothers you."

"No, we have to learn to live here in Moonbeam with him. And Lacey. Yes, I know she has a name." Her eyes flickered with ire, but then her mouth slipped into a small smile. "She probably wants to book The Destiny because you do all the work, the food, the entertainment. She just has to show up on Father's arm."

"Probably." And Heather was right. This party might lead to more bookings for him. But he'd turn all that down if it bothered her, because there was no way he ever wanted to get back on bad footing with Heather. He'd missed her too much. Way too much. Sometimes so much it caught him off guard, like when something good happened and he wanted to reach for his phone to call her and tell her.

He fervently hoped they were getting back to that stage. That they could just erase the last few years of discord.

Tally came over to the table, interrupting his thoughts. "So it looks like the island is going to provide you with one of our signature sunsets tonight."

"It does." Heather glanced out at the view.

"I'm really glad you two decided to come tonight. It's not often I see people from Moonbeam these days, what with The Cabot reopened—and I hear its dining room is fabulous—and the opening of Parker Cafe."

"Don't let Livy hear you call it that. Its official name is Sea Glass Cafe." Heather laughed. "But no one in the town calls it that."

"I'll have to get over to Moonbeam and try it out. You know, that and take a cruise on The Destiny." Tally smiled ruefully. "But it seems like I'm always so busy here."

"You're welcome on The Destiny anytime. And I'm sure they'd love to have you at the cafe, too." Jesse said. But he sure could relate to the always being too busy to do some of the things he'd love to do.

"Here comes your server. I'll let you two eat. Enjoy your meal." Tally smiled and whisked away to chat with a couple at a nearby table.

"I've missed this place," Heather said as their server placed their meal on the table.

He looked at the mouthwatering dinners. "I have, too." And he'd missed just the simple pleasure of having a meal with Heather.

CHAPTER 12

They left Magic Cafe after having a wonderful dinner, watching a spectacular sunset, and chatting with Tally again for a bit. Heather couldn't remember the last time she'd had such a nice, relaxing evening. And one with Jesse, on top of that.

As they headed over the bridge and back toward Moonbeam, Jesse sang along softly to a song on the radio. She'd forgotten how he'd do that. Join in on parts of the song, his deep voice following along with the melody. He knew all the words to about a bazillion songs as near as she could figure.

He glanced over at her as they pulled into Moonbeam. "So, would you like to come over to my cottage for a bit? We could have a drink out on the deck. It's sure nice out tonight—" He paused, and she wasn't sure if he was finished or not. "And I'm not ready for the evening to end."

She swore she could hear him holding his breath, waiting for her answer.

What was her answer? She debated a moment or two. The evening had been nice. Very nice. Should she chance ruining it by spending even more time with him? But the thing was, she *wanted* to spend more time with him. Like when they were kids, and it was just never enough time together. Best friends. Constant companions.

"I'd like that." There. The decision was made. Besides, she was a bit curious to see inside his cottage. He'd moved since the last time she'd been to his place. That time when Shelly had been there... She put the thought aside.

They pulled into the drive at his cottage and got out. She followed him up the steps to his front door and he opened it, flicking on the lights as they entered. She looked around, taking it all in. The cottage was an open concept design, and she could see all the way through to the view out the French doors lining the beachside of the house. The kitchen was tucked over to one side. He'd furnished the house with a comfortable-looking sofa and overstuffed chairs. She walked further into the house and stopped, staring at the wall.

She pointed to the wall hanging. "You have one of my illustrations." She stepped closer. It was a signed copy. "It looks like... one of my originals?"

He nodded. "I searched around until I found a gallery that sold some of your original artwork. I wanted a Heather Parker original." He flashed an impish grin. "Since I couldn't have the real person."

Shock swept through her. Even with everything that happened between them, he'd paid for an original piece of her artwork. And she knew he'd paid a pretty penny for it, too. "I would have *given* you an original if you'd asked."

"Ah, but we weren't exactly speaking at the time." His easy smile teased her gently.

"I guess there was that."

He led her through the cottage, grabbed a bottle of wine and two glasses, and they headed out to his deck. The almost-but-not-quite full moon spilled light down across the water. A palm tree flickered shadows on the sand. Stars danced above them as they sat down on a glider and looked out at the rolling waves.

The glider slid slowly back and forth, and she found herself mesmerized by the moment. Together with Jesse again. Comfortable with him. Talking about anything and everything.

Friends again? Maybe.

Could that really happen?

Jesse draped his arm around Heather's shoulder, and she leaned against him. He didn't miss the tiny sigh that escaped her lips. It felt so right to be back on good terms with her. Phenomenal, stupendous, exceptional, even. And any other word he could think of.

He'd made so many mistakes over the years with her. So many. Saying things he didn't mean. Telling her what he thought she wanted to hear. Afraid of chasing her away if he told her how he really felt.

Now that he was older, though, it seemed foolish to deny his feelings. And he'd give anything to see if they could figure out what they really meant to each other. He just knew he didn't want to lose her from his life again.

And yet... there was one thing he wanted to do. He set down his drink on the table beside him and took her hand. "You know what, Heather Parker?"

She looked up and gave him a small questioning smile. But he could see something in her eyes. Probably the same thing she could see in his. A connection. A definite connection.

"There's something I'd like to do. But I've learned my lesson. I don't want to surprise you."

She licked her lips and swallowed before saying anything. "And what is it you want to do?" But her face said she knew exactly what he was thinking. But of course, she did. She could read his mind, he'd swear it.

"I'd like to kiss you if that's okay. No surprises this time." He tucked a flyaway lock of hair behind her ear and held his breath, hoping he'd chosen the right time to take a chance. Then when she didn't answer, he wondered if he'd blown it. Ruined the fragile closeness that they'd found again.

"I think—" She bit her bottom lip and looked away from him, staring out at the water.

He'd messed up. So much for being older and wiser. His heart plummeted.

She turned back to him. "I think I'd like that. A lot."

His heart somersaulted, and he reached over and gently cupped her face. "Ah, Heather. Let me get it right this time." He leaned closer and gently kissed those lips that he'd been staring at all night. Wondering what they'd feel like under his again after all these years.

Her hand slipped around his neck and he deepened the kiss as wave after wave of emotion flowed over him like the surf upon the shore, drowning him and yet saving him at the same time.

Heather clung to Jesse's shoulders as if grabbing a lifeline. His kiss rocked her to her very soul as a cacophony of thoughts erupted in her mind. Her heart pounded so hard, she could scarcely breathe. Still, she clung to him. It had been a million years since she'd felt his lips on hers. Since he'd touched her face. Since...

No matter how much she'd denied it over the years, she'd longed for his kisses. But she'd made so many mistakes with him. So many choices that hadn't turned out like she'd planned.

He finally pulled back, and she opened her eyes to see him still inches from her, a lopsided grin on his face. "That was nice, Heather Parker."

"It—was..." She struggled to take in a deep breath of the salty air and calm herself. Would her heart ever settle back to a normal rhythm?

But Jesse gave her no time. He leaned in for another kiss. Then another. They sat out on the deck long into the night. Talking. Kissing. Holding hands. Catching up on everything that had happened to both of them in the last few years.

Although a clench of her heart reminded her that she hadn't told him everything. Some things were just too hard to tell, to explain. She'd tell him someday.

Maybe.

Probably.

No, for sure she would.

But for now, she just wanted to revel in the emotions of the night. She'd sort out all her feelings soon. Go home and overthink things like she always did. But not tonight. Tonight she was just going to enjoy the kisses. Enjoy his fingers entwined with hers. It was enough just sitting with her head resting on his broad shoulder and feeling his fingers stroke her cheek.

And tonight, she hoped neither of them ended the night by saying it was a mistake. Because that's what had started all the trouble between them...

CHAPTER 13

Jesse looked down at Heather, sound asleep, tucked up against his side. Tonight had been more than he'd ever imagined he'd have with her. And he sure wasn't going to ruin things this time. There had been no surprise kiss. And he sure wasn't going to say this had been a mistake. Because it wasn't. Just a slow, easy evening. Kisses and talk. He could feel the dopey smile spreading across his face and didn't care. He was happy. So very happy and content. Like pieces of his life were finally starting to fall into place.

She stirred in his arms, opened her eyes, and looked up. A sleepy smile crossed her reddened lips. "Sorry, I guess I nodded off."

"It is getting late. Or should I say early? See, the sky is beginning to lighten."

She looked at her watch. "Goodness. We sat here talking all night long."

"And kissing," he reminded her.

"And that."

"I should take you home." But he hoped she'd disagree.

"Yes, I guess you should." She sat up and stretched, then rose from the glider.

He took her hand, and they walked through the cottage and out toward his car. She turned to him. "You think we could walk?"

"I'd like that very much." Anything to delay the moment of her leaving him.

They held hands and walked through the streets of Moonbeam, passing no one, in and out of the light of the streetlamps, as the sky continued to lighten.

He dropped her off at the lobby of her condo, kissing her again, and turned to walk back home. Alone with his thoughts, he reviewed every moment of the night. The kisses. The look in her eyes. The way she felt so right in his arms.

Could he really be lucky enough to have a second chance with Heather Parker?

Heather sat on the balcony of her condo, not quite ready to go to sleep. Not quite ready to call it a night. Although actually, it was almost morning. Soon the sun would burst above the horizon. A new day would begin.

She reached up and touched her lips and smiled. So many kisses. Some gentle, some filled with desire and need. Her emotions swirled around her, but one thing, one emotion, was clear. She cared about Jesse. She always had. But could they really become more than friends?

She guessed they'd crossed that line tonight, anyway. The more than friends line.

She rose and paced back and forth on the balcony. But if they were going to work things out, see how things progressed between them... then they shouldn't have any secrets. She stared out into the distance as the sun began to pink up the sky, hoping the sunrise would give her answers.

But her heart knew what she had to do. Needed to do. She'd tell him tomorrow. He'd understand.

Maybe.

Or it might ruin everything.

Okay, maybe she wouldn't tell him tomorrow. Well, today, since it was daylight already. She'd like a few more days of this peacefulness with him. This truce. This rightness. But she'd tell him soon. And all she could do is hope he'd understand.

She had the wildest desire to call Livy and explain everything to her. Talk things through. Get her advice on the best way to tell Jesse. But it was way too early to be calling her cousin. And she wasn't certain she was ready to tell Livy either.

She sighed and turned to go inside and try to get a few hours of sleep. With one last look out at the bay, she slid the door closed behind her.

At least this time, at the end of the night, Jesse hadn't said it was all a mistake. Not like last time, when he'd said it and shattered her heart.

CHAPTER 14

The next day Jesse opened the door to his cottage to find a boy, maybe about Emily's age—although he wasn't very good at guessing kids' ages—standing on the front step. "Can I help you?"

"Are you—are you Jesse Brown?" A gleam of curiosity hovered in the boy's eyes, and he quickly bit his lip.

"Yes." He leaned against the doorjamb, wondering what the boy wanted. Maybe selling something? Was it candy selling time, or a wrapping paper fundraising, or...?

"I've been looking for you." The boy shifted carefully from foot to foot, and a battered backpack slipped from his shoulder to the ground. He had on worn shorts, a t-shirt with some band name on it that he didn't recognize, and scuffed up tennis shoes that had seen better days.

"Looking for me? What for?"

"Have you lived here forever?"

Curious question. "Yes, all my life."

"Are there other Jesse Browns in Moonbeam?"

"Not that I've heard of." He narrowed his eyes as a sense of wariness enveloped him. "What's this about?"

The boy looked up, a mask of protectiveness firmly held across his features as he gulped a large breath of air. "I think that—at least I'm pretty sure—" His tone was overly nonchalant if a bit tinged with something.

Apprehension?

"What's this about?" He repeated his question. He could tell the boy was nervous, but he needed to get to the point or they'd stand in the doorway all day.

The boy licked his lips, squared his shoulders, then stared directly at him. "I think you're my father." The words came out in a rush, and the boy looked at him with an expression of defiance mixed with undeniable hope.

Jesse's breath caught, and he searched the boy's face, looking for... something. Some sign of himself in the boy. Okay, so he had blue eyes that had turned the same shade of steel blue that his did when he was angry or stressed. Coincidence. He had thick blonde hair like his own. But seriously, how many people in the world had blue eyes and blonde hair?

And... well... he *didn't have a son.*

The boy stood there, a wary look on his face, watching his every move.

"I don't have a son," he stated the obvious.

"I'm pretty sure you're the right Jesse Brown," he insisted, his voice quavering just a bit.

"What makes you think I'm your father?" Was he really even having this conversation? The absurdity of the situation left him flabbergasted. If anyone used that word anymore. But it sure fit *this* situation.

"Because I found a letter that said you were my father and you lived in Moonbeam. I found it in my mother's things after—" The boy paused and pain flashed through his eyes before he quickly hid it and the mask of exaggerated nonchalance settled on his face again. "After my mother died."

"I'm sorry." His answer was automatic. That's what you said when someone told them their mom died.

The boy nodded.

Jesse asked the obvious question. "And who was your mother?"

"Christina Lee."

Ah ha. He'd never met a Christina Lee in his life. Nor a Chris Lee or Tina Lee or any other variation he could come up with. Relief swept through him. Kind of. The boy was obviously upset.

"I don't know a Christina Lee," he explained patiently, halfway sorry for bursting the boy's bubble and crushing his hopes.

The boy looked at him for a long moment. "Christina Lee was my adopted mom. I mean, I was adopted."

"Oh." He stared at him, still trying to sort all this out. "And where's your father? I mean the one who adopted you."

"I never knew him. He died before I was one year old."

"I'm sorry." There it was again. Automatic.

"But I found all this information hidden in a box in my mother's things." He leaned down and pulled out a wad of documents. "The box had the paperwork for the adoption and my original birth certificate."

He cocked his head to one side and took a deep breath. "And who is listed as your mother? Your *birth* mother?"

The boy looked right into his eyes. "Heather Carlson. But I can't find her."

He slumped against the doorframe. "Heather Carlson?" *His* Heather? Heather Parker, formerly known as Heather Carlson...

"You know her, right? I've found the right Jesse Brown?" His eyes filled with hope.

"I know her..." A whirlwind of surprise and anger and incredulity churned inside him. He sucked in a deep breath and stared at the boy. Then he stood up straight, stepped aside, and motioned to him. "You should probably come inside."

The boy picked up his backpack and walked into his home. This boy that might be... that *probably* was his son?

He clenched his teeth. Heather had a lot of explaining to do. A *whole lot* of explaining.

CHAPTER 15

J esse followed the boy into the cottage and
stopped. The boy. He couldn't keep
thinking of him as *the boy*. And they
needed to talk. "Ah, would you like a soda or
something?"

"Yeah, sure." He set the backpack on the
floor but still clutched the papers in his hand.

Jesse went into the kitchen, poured them
sodas, and came back to find him standing and
staring out the window. "Here."

He nodded thanks and turned to look out
the window again. "You have a great view. Must
be nice living on the beach."

"It is. You want to go sit out on the deck?
We should talk."

They went outside, and the boy sat on the

edge of a chair, alternating between looking at him and quickly looking back out at the water. Jesse set his drink on a table and turned to the boy. "I don't even know your name."

"Blake."

He rolled the name over in his head. Blake. It seemed to fit him. Well, as much as he knew about the boy, which was exactly... nothing. Okay, so he knew his name and his mother's name. And the fact both his parents were dead.

Only that wasn't the truth. Both of his parents—he and Heather—were very much alive. *If* all of this was true.

But it couldn't be. Because Heather wouldn't have done this. Given up a child. *His* child. Without a word to him.

"Where do you live?" He suddenly wanted to know everything about Blake. Every detail of his life.

"I live in Lawrence, Kansas now. With my aunt. Only... she doesn't really like having me live there."

He frowned. "Does she know you're here?"

Blake looked down at his scuffed shoes, then up at him defiantly. "Not exactly. She thinks I'm visiting my best friend in Nashville. That's where I lived with my mom. My aunt let me take a bus to Nashville and my friend covered for me so I could get another bus and come down here. Anyway, my aunt was headed on a long cruise with her new boyfriend. She was glad to have a place to... dump me."

His mind spun and whirled with all the questions he had. "How long has your mom been... uh... gone?"

"Nine months."

"How old are you?"

"Fifteen."

He did the math and gritted his teeth. There was every possibility that Blake was telling the truth.

Because just one time in the history of his and Heather's friendship...

That one night that she'd been so upset and he'd comforted her...

That one night they'd slept together...

And they'd both agreed it was a mistake never to be repeated. And it hadn't.

But this? Anger and disbelief swept through him. Heather would not have kept something like this from him. She wouldn't. She *couldn't*.

But as he stared at Blake and watched him nervously drum his fingers on the arm of the chair, he was starting to realize that maybe all this was the truth. The twisted, cruel, and unbelievable truth.

"Here, look at these." Blake thrust the paperwork toward him.

He took the papers and paged through them. A birth certificate with Heather's name on it along with his. He glanced at the adoption papers with signatures and legal notarizations.

"It was a private adoption," Blake explained. "I think Mom said it was through someone she knew from church. They knew this Heather woman who didn't want her kid."

He winced at the words, then looked at the last piece of paper. His heart clutched as he recognized the handwriting.

"My mom... *birth* mother... she wrote that letter to me."

There was just no way to deny the truth. He scanned the letter Heather had written. Saying she loved the boy, but this was for the best and she hoped he had a wonderful life. A bit detached in the wording, but a few words of explanation.

"She left me this necklace." Blake slipped a necklace from the pocket of his backpack and fingered a necklace with a silver sand dollar hanging from it. "I don't know why. It's not like a guy would wear it."

He closed his eyes. He'd bet anything there was an inscription on the back.

"It says..."

He held up a hand. "To my beloved Grace. And the date is February 14, 1926."

Blake's eyes widened. "How did you know?"

"I've... I've seen it before." Many, many years ago. A family heirloom that Heather had treasured.

"So are you beginning to believe me?"

"I am." He nodded. "I want you to know that I didn't know anything about you." His voice was low, quiet, subdued. So many thoughts. He set the papers on the table, closed his eyes for a moment, then opened them and stared at Blake. "I knew...nothing." Pain seared through his heart at all he'd missed. All he hadn't known.

The boy searched his face for a moment, then nodded. "Okay. Would you have kept me if you *did* know about me?"

"I..." He paused and thought about it. "Yes. I mean, I think so. I hope so. I can't imagine giving up my own child." Though that was exactly what Heather did. Without saying a word to him. Without giving him any choice.

"So... could you help me now?" Blake's face still clasped onto its protective mask, but his eyes held a tiny bit of hope. "Because I heard my aunt say that she was thinking of turning me over to the state. That it was just too hard to raise me. And I cost her too much money." A dash of pain flitted across his eyes again, but just as quickly disappeared. "But I don't ask for things. Not a phone, or new clothes, or anything. I don't cause her much trouble. I don't. I do good in school. I help clean and I know how to cook."

Jesse stared at Blake, trying to plead his case, asserting that he was a good kid. His heart clutched in his chest.

Blake continued, "But I've heard about those places that they send kids my age that no one wants. I... I don't want to go there. So, I thought maybe you could help me get emancipated. I know it will cost some money. I'll pay you back. I swear. I'll be sixteen soon and that's what I want." His voice was assured and confident.

He sat back in his chair, stunned. All Blake had gone through. Losing his father, his mother, and now his aunt didn't want him. And all he wanted was to be emancipated? To be on his own.

He was way too young for that.

"I tell you what. We're going to figure this all out. You and me, okay? I'm going to have to talk to a lawyer and sort through all this."

"Really, you'll help me?" Blake's eyes widened in surprise.

"Yes, of course, I'll help you."

"Thank you." A tentative smile flickered across Blake's lips, then he frowned. "So... this Heather. My mom. What's she like? Do you ever see her?"

In an act of incredible fate, or maybe the universe laughing at all of them, he heard a voice calling from inside. "Jesse? You home?"

Heather.

Anger swept through him with such intensity that he couldn't even think straight. He clenched his fists. He glanced at Blake. "Out here."

Heather came to the open door, a wide, just-for-him smile on her face. Then she saw Blake and nodded at him. "Hello there. Didn't know Jesse had company."

Blake shifted uneasily in his chair.

It looked like this was the day for shocks for everyone. He looked over at Blake, hoping the boy could take yet another surprise because he was suddenly very protective of him.

"Blake... ah... this is... Heather. Heather, this is your son, Blake."

All the color drained from Heather's face, and she gasped as she grabbed the doorframe.

CHAPTER 16

Heather held onto the doorframe as if it would stop her whole life from exploding around her. Staring at the boy and then Jesse with his words swirling through her mind. She shut her eyes and took a deep breath. For a moment the world went out of focus before slowly clearing again. She opened her eyes and couldn't take her gaze off the boy.

Blake.

Her son. How many years had she dreamed of him? Dreamed of actually meeting him.

But not like this. Definitely not like this.

"I was just telling Blake about how I had no idea about him. Didn't know he existed. Didn't know I had a child."

She couldn't miss the cutting, icy tone in his words.

"I—" She tore her gaze from Blake to look at Jesse. His face held back barely controlled fury, his eyes a stormy steel blue.

Blake stood and took a tentative step toward her. "You're really my mom? Heather Carlson?"

"She goes by Heather *Parker* now." Jesse said the words automatically and tilted his head, watching her.

"Oh," Blake said as he stood awkwardly in front of her.

Heather tried to pull herself together enough to say something. Anything. She swept her gaze over the boy and her heart crumbled into a million pieces. Her son. The one she'd missed every single day of her life. The one she often talked to silently in her mind. The one she scanned the streets for, wondering if some young boy would catch her eye and she'd just *know* he was her son.

"Blake." She said the boy's name, trying it on.

"Uh, hi." Blake stood as if waiting for something, then he slid his hands into his pockets and took a step back.

Heather was torn between rushing forward

and hugging him and just... touching him. His face. After all these years. But still she stood, grasping the doorframe, afraid she'd fall.

The boy was slim, and she wasn't sure if that was from not eating enough or one of those awkward growth spurts kids got. He was in need of a haircut, and his clothes were clean but worn. He had a tiny, almost unnoticeable scar at the side of his forehead. But she noticed. She noticed every single detail about him. She couldn't get enough.

And he had Jesse's eyes. No denying that.

"I—" She stared at her hand. Why wouldn't her hand reach out? She needed to touch him, make sure he was real, right here in front of her.

Blake gave a small shrug as if expecting nothing from her and went back to sit on the edge of his chair, grabbing his soda and taking a large swallow.

She should follow and tug him to his feet and hug him...

"Blake's mom died," Jesse said, his tone still frigid.

"Oh, I'm sorry."

"I mean, *you're* not dead. Obviously. The woman who adopted him died. You know, from when you gave him up for adoption. Without telling me anything about him." His tone was controlled and even. *Overly* controlled.

But she knew Jesse. Knew him too well. He was way past angry. And she couldn't blame him. Because she had kept this secret. For all these years. There was no excuse for that. None.

Just then Livy and Austin climbed up the stairs to the deck. "Hey, we were out walking and saw you guys up here—" Livy stopped short and stared at Heather. "You okay? You're really pale."

"I—"

"She's in a bit of shock," Jesse explained. "She just met her son."

Livy whirled around and stared at Blake. "Her... what? *Son?*"

"You didn't know about him either?" Jesse's eyes blazed. "Ah, another Heather Parker secret."

"Jesse, please," she whispered.

Livy shook her head, and her wounded look tore at Heather's heart. But Liv would have to stand in line. So many people were hurt right now.

"Blake, this would be... I don't know the right term. But this is your mother's cousin.

She's some relation to you." Jesse's eyes bore into Heather before turning back to Blake.

"Hi," Blake said politely. "Nice to meet you."

Livy reached out and touched Blake's shoulder, giving him a warm smile. "It's really nice to meet you."

Which is what she should have done. Touched him. Wrapped him in her arms. The arms that had missed him since the day the social worker had taken him out of her arms and given him to his adopted mother.

Livy sank into a chair, a stunned look on her face. Austin moved to stand beside her, resting his hand on her arm. He shot Jesse a questioning look, and Jesse just shrugged.

"A lot of people didn't know about you, Blake," Jesse explained, his voice gentle and kind in quite the contrast to the tone he was using with her. "I'm so sorry about that."

"I didn't mean to cause... trouble."

"No, son. None of this is your fault," Jesse assured the boy. "I'm glad you came to find me. And I'll do anything to help you. I promise."

Jesse turned to Livy. "So, I'm clueless about all this and I guess you are too, Livy. I'll explain everything later, but he's found us. He has the birth certificate. And... let's say I did some math, and it's quite possible what he's saying is the truth."

Livy looked from Jesse and back to her. Then she looked over at the table beside Blake and gasped. "Is that... Is that Grace's sand dollar necklace? Heather, you said you lost it."

Heather looked from Livy, to Blake, to Jesse, and the world whirled out of focus again before becoming all too crystal clear. She nodded. "Yes, it's Grace's necklace. I left it with his mother to give to him. I wanted him to have *something* of our family's."

Livy rose and walked over to her. "You had a child, and you never told me?"

She wasn't sure if there was more hurt in Livy's eyes or her voice. "I... yes." What else was there to say? And one look at Blake and anyone could see he was Jesse's son. Those eyes.

Livy turned her face and looked out at the ocean before looking back at her, but she didn't ask any more questions.

Jesse stood and walked over to lean against the railing, his white-knuckled grip as he clutched the wood betraying his barely contained anger. "But now we need to sort things out. I told Blake I'd talk to a lawyer. His parents—the ones who adopted him—are gone. They've passed away. He lives with his aunt, and it seems his aunt isn't pleased with the arrangement. Blake came here to see if I'd help him get emancipated. He's not too keen on being shipped to the state group home for foster kids."

"Does she know Blake is here?" Livy asked.

"No... she thinks he's at a friend's house in Nashville."

Livy turned to Blake. "You need to call your aunt and tell her where you are."

"She's out of the country. On a cruise."

"You still should try to get a message to her."

Austin stepped forward. "Jesse, you could talk to Delbert. He knows everyone. He might have a recommendation of a lawyer for you."

Jesse nodded. "Good idea. I'll do that first thing in the morning."

Heather watched them all talking around her. Taking in the words, but not fully comprehending. Jesse was going to get a lawyer to what?

"Blake, you look like you've had a long day. How about I get you set up in my guest room?

We'll try to get a message to your aunt. Then I'll cook us a nice big dinner."

"I can stay here?" Blake's eyes widened, flooding with hope. "You sure? I won't be any trouble."

Heather's heart clutched again. He was so grateful for a place to stay. A kindness offered to him.

What had she done?

She thought she'd been doing the right thing by giving him up for adoption. She'd been nineteen, alone, and knew nothing about being a mother. She sure hadn't had a role model in the parenting department.

But what kind of life had Blake had? He had no one now.

But *she'd* wanted him. She had wanted him so badly. Loved him so deeply. Deeply enough to give him to someone who could give him a better life. Thinking of what he *needed* more than what she *wanted*. Only... now...

Jesse interrupted her thoughts. "You should go now, Heather."

"But—"

"No. You should go." Jesse pushed away from the railing and stared at her with a don't-you-dare-argue look on his face.

"Come on, Heather. We'll walk you home." Livy took her arm. She stared down at Livy's hand on her arm.

"But—"

"No, Jesse is right. Let Blake have some time to settle in. Jesse can start sorting things out legally." Livy swiveled her gaze between her and Jesse. "And then you two need to talk."

She turned to Blake, uncertain what to say. She dropped to her knees in front of him and looked into his eyes. "I'm so glad to see you again. After all these years. I've... missed you."

"You have?" Blake's widened in surprise.

"Every single minute of every single day." She touched his hand gently, and the force of emotion almost knocked her across the deck. Finally, touching his hand again after all these years.

"Heather." Jesse's cold single word cut through her memories.

She smiled encouragingly at Blake and nodded, then rose to her feet. She followed Livy and Austin down the stairs to the beach, looking back over her shoulder and watching as Jesse and Blake disappeared inside the cottage.

Blake. Her son.

CHAPTER 17

Olivia walked beside her cousin as they left Jesse's. Heather trudged without speaking, without looking at her. Livy wanted to say something but had no idea what to say. She was still in shock that Heather had a son and had never told her. They told each other *everything*.

Or maybe they didn't.

They headed down the beach until Heather stopped under a group of palm trees and sank onto the sand, burying her face in her hands.

Livy stopped and stared at her cousin. She'd never, ever in her whole life seen her cousin cry. But sobs were coming from her now. Deep, heartfelt sobs.

Austin leaned close and whispered, "I'll let

you two talk. Call me if you need me." He touched her face gently, then turned and headed down the beach toward his cottage.

She sank onto the sand beside Heather and wrapped her arm around her cousin's shoulders, letting her cry. Huge sobs escaped Heather and her shoulders heaved. She finally got her crying semi under control and dashed her hand across her tear-streaked face. "I've really messed it up this time, haven't I?"

"I... Yes, I think you have." She hugged her. "I love you. You know that. But... to keep this from Jesse?"

"And you."

"And me. I admit it. That hurts. I thought we knew everything about each other."

"I know, but—"

"I didn't even know you'd ever slept with Jesse."

"It was only one time. Right after Emily was born. Remember I came to town to see her?"

She nodded, then frowned. "But then you left in a hurry."

"Right. Because of Jesse. The next morning —after we slept together—he said it had been a mistake. So I agreed with him. What else could I say? Then after I left, I found out I was pregnant." A sob escaped Heather again. "And what did I know about being a mom? And I was nineteen. I didn't have a mother like yours who would step in and help."

"You don't know that." Though her cousin was probably right. Heather's mother had never been very maternal, even though Aunt Evelyn and Heather had started to improve their relationship in the last few months.

Heather swiped at her tears again. "Jesse was struggling to get through college and save up money for his dream of owning his own business. How could I drop more responsibility on him? I know what he would have done. He would have dropped out of college and taken on another job." Heather closed her eyes. "And I didn't want him to be with me because of the baby. I wanted him to... *want* to be with me."

"I'm sure it was a hard decision to make. And you can't change it now. But it seems like the boy is in kind of a rough spot now."

"I wanted to give him a good life. In a normal family. My family was never normal. And Father would never have accepted the baby into the family. Or accepted Jesse for that matter."

"Probably not." She agreed. "But I would have helped you. Mom would have."

Heather looked directly at her. "I honestly thought I was doing the best thing for everyone. For... Blake. For Jesse. Just not for me... I've missed him every day of my life. It's like there's a huge hole in my heart that I've never been able to fill."

"So, what are you going to do about that?"

Heather gulped out a rasping laugh. "You're a tough one."

"So?"

"So, I'm going to talk to Jesse. And I'll see what I can do to help legally. I can't let Blake be sent to foster care in a group home. I can't. I wanted to give him the best life... not this. And I want to get to know him."

"You're going to have to take it slow with Blake." She patted Heather's arm. "And with Jesse? There's a chance he won't forgive you. Not something this big. You have to be prepared for that."

"I know." Heather scooped up a handful of sand and let it sift out between her fingers. "But I'm going to try to make it up to everyone." She stared down at her fingers and the sand slipping through them. "Not that I really ever can... I feel like such a fraud. Such a failure."

The tortured pain in Heather's voice tore at Olivia's heart. But there wasn't much she could do to help Heather now. She was going to have to figure this out for herself.

Heather stood out on the balcony of her condo, staring mindlessly out over the bay. She barely noticed the sky putting on a spectacular display of moonlight and star shine. It did nothing to soothe her. Nothing.

She paced from one end of the balcony to the other. Restless. Hurting. Confused.

How could something she did that she thought was *so right*—all those years ago—turn out so badly?

She had to stop herself from going over to Jesse's tonight. She wanted to see Blake again. Ask him questions. Hear about his life. Touch his hand again. She remembered the last time she'd touched his hand before he'd been taken away. He'd been so small, and he'd curled his tiny fingers around one of hers. The memory was seared into her brain, into her very being.

Tears began to roll down her cheeks again. Tears. She didn't cry. It just wasn't something she did. Not even the day she'd handed Blake over to his new mother.

All the pain of that day swept over her like a rogue wave. Blake's adopted parents had seemed perfect. They were so in love and had tried for years to have a child of their own. Someone she'd worked with knew them, and when Heather had finally confided she was thinking of giving the baby up for adoption, she'd been put in contact with them.

Had they been kind to Blake? Been good parents? Had he had a good life up until he'd lost his mom? All these questions. What was his favorite subject in school? Did he play sports? What foods did he like? Music? Books?

A knock at the door drew her attention, and she headed through the condo to answer it, swiping away tears as she walked.

"Mom."

Her mother took one look at her and gathered her into her arms. "Oh, Heather."

She clung to her mother, wondering when the last time was that they'd hugged like this.

Had they ever?

Her mother finally stepped back and

reached over and brushed her hair away from her face. "I heard from Livy. I hope that's okay she told me. She was so upset when she came to the cafe. Sad, too."

"Oh, Mom. It's all such a mess. Jesse is so mad, and I don't blame him."

"Come on. Let me make us tea. You sit." Her mother led them into the kitchen and put on the teakettle. She bustled around making the tea, then sat down beside her at the small cafe table.

"Okay, now talk to me. So, you had a child."

"I did. Sixteen years ago."

Her mother sighed. "So you were only about nineteen? So young. And... well, I remember how things were then. Really bad between you and your father. You'd moved out and lived far away."

"I didn't think I could be a good mother."

Sadness hovered in her mother's eyes. "Because I was never a good mother."

"Mom, don't say that."

"But I wasn't. I should have stood up to your father more. He was... horrible to you."

"But it was always easier to just take what he said and did instead of standing up to him. It just made things worse."

"That's no excuse. I should have done better. I'm the mother. I have so many regrets." Her mother's eyes filled with pain. "I'm sorry I wasn't a better mother to you."

"I have regrets, too. I should have tried more to keep in touch with you, even though I didn't want to see Father. And... I've regretted giving up my son every day since the day I did. Though I thought I was doing the right thing. Giving him a better life. One... different than mine."

"Oh, Heather. I'm sorry. I take responsibility for your decision, too. If I'd been more like Donna, you would have felt like you could have come to me for help. You were all alone and so young."

"But... I know it was wrong not to tell Jesse. He should have had some say in the decision. It's just... I know Jesse. He would have insisted I keep the baby. And I don't think that Jesse and I, at barely twenty, would have given the baby —his name is Blake, did Livy tell you that—we couldn't have provided him with a very good life. And Jesse would have dropped out of school. We had no money. And Father would have... he would have made it difficult, if not impossible, to live here in Moonbeam. And Jesse loves Moonbeam. It's part of him. I just wanted to give my son the best life possible. A normal life."

"I'm sure you did what you thought was best for Blake." Her mother reached over and squeezed her hand. "I just wish... I wish things had been different. That I had been different."

"Oh, Mom, you should see Blake. He's a good-looking kid. Skinny. He has Jesse's blue eyes and blonde hair. And he's taller than I am."

"I can't wait to meet him."

Heather sat back. That's right, her mother now had a grandson she'd known nothing about. Her decision had affected so many people. Not the least, Jesse. And Blake.

"I want to try and make things right now." She let out a long sigh. "But how in the world am I ever going to do that?"

"You start by talking to Jesse and Blake."

Jesse gave up on trying to sleep. He'd tossed and turned for hours. He crawled out of bed and padded barefoot down the hallway. He couldn't resist peeking in on Blake.

The boy was sprawled across the bed, his

blanket a tangle around him. He looked peaceful in sleep, younger than his years. Jesse resisted the urge to go over and push his hair back from his eyes. He didn't want to chance waking him up. He marveled that this perfect person was part of him. His son. He still couldn't get used to the idea, but he had to admit he was pretty pleased with it. He never thought he'd have a child... and now he did. Not a child exactly, but a young man.

Blake's backpack was dumped in the corner with its few possessions spilled out on the floor. He'd deal with that today, too. Take him shopping for more clothes. And he'd have to get more groceries. The boy could eat. He'd gobbled down dinner along with a dessert or three, then a snack before bed.

He wandered out to the deck and sat in the moonlight. Barely controlled anger washed through him, wave after wave. He clenched his teeth just thinking about Heather and this awful thing she'd done to him. To Blake.

The anger was mixed with sadness for all he'd missed in Blake's life. His first words, first steps, being able to teach him how to throw a ball or how to fish.

They'd tried to get ahold of Blake's aunt

yesterday and finally left a message. He wondered how that was going to work out when she finally received it. And he had to talk to a lawyer first thing. So many uncertainties.

Well, there was *one* certainty. He was going to do everything in his power to help the boy, and if at all possible, he wanted Blake to move here and live with him. Father and son. Like it should have been all along.

CHAPTER 18

Heather hurried into Sea Glass Cafe as soon as it opened. She had something she just *had* to do. First she picked up some of Evelyn's cinnamon rolls. A growing boy had to eat, didn't he?

"You going to take these over to Jesse's?" Livy asked as she boxed up the rolls.

"I am. Don't know if he'll accept them, but I'm going to try. I need to shop a bit at the general store first, too."

"Good luck talking to Jesse and Blake today." Livy gave her an encouraging smile. Which was good, because she needed all the encouragement and support she could get.

"Thanks, I'll need it."

She crossed into the general store and looked around, uncertain what she was after. She knew nothing about Blake, really. She picked out a t-shirt that said Moonbeam Bay on it, hoping she'd guessed the right size. Then a pocketknife, because didn't all boys like those? Then she second-guessed herself. Was a pocketknife an acceptable gift? But she could remember Jesse carving things out of driftwood when they were kids.

Okay, she'd get the pocketknife and quit dithering on her decision.

She'd also carefully wrapped up a drawing of hers that she'd had for years. A small, blonde-haired boy playing in the waves. It had been her dream of what he might be like. And now... Would she get a chance to go to the beach with him? Walk on the shore. Play in the waves. Go shelling. Simple things. Things a mother would do with her son.

She got a card after wavering back and forth on which one to buy, then grabbed a gift bag and went to check out.

"Morning," Aunt Donna greeted her, eyeing the purchases.

"Yes, they are for Blake."

Donna eyed the card, and her eyes widened. "Really?"

She just nodded and fought back tears. Tears. Where were they coming from? She wanted to get back to her normal, never-crying self.

After carefully packaging up her gifts, she drove over to Jesse's. She sat in her vehicle, her old, beloved teal jeep, grasping the steering wheel as if it could impart some magic courage to her. With a deep breath of resolution, she opened the door, grabbed the print, the gift bag, and the bribe—*she meant cinnamon rolls*—and walked up to Jesse's door.

He opened it on the first knock and stood there in silence, as cold as a polar bear plunge in frigid water. Not that she'd ever done one, but she bet it held nothing on Jesse's look.

"I... brought these." She shoved the box of cinnamon rolls toward him.

He looked at the box without taking it. It was obvious what they were, with *Sea Glass Cafe* stamped onto the box and the clear cellophane window on top. Her heart sank. He wasn't going to make this easy, but then she hadn't expected him to.

"And then..." She paused, gathering her

nerve. "I got these for Blake." She held out the gift bag and the wrapped print.

"He doesn't need anything from you. You can't buy your way into his life. Bringing presents? Do you think that will help? You gave him up. You already made your decision on whether you wanted him to be a part of your life." His eyes flashed a steely blue and his jaw clenched tight.

"Jesse, don't be like that." A stab of scalding pain tore at her heart.

"Like what? Protective of my son? You know, now that I even know he exists."

"We need to talk." She said it as firmly as she could under the icy glare emanating from him.

"No, we don't." His voice was just as firm.

She wavered under the fierce anger in his eyes. "I—" She paused and took a deep breath. "Can you please just give these to him? It's important."

"Why is it so important?" He stood with his arms folded across his chest.

"Because... Because today... Because today is his birthday."

Jesse's eyes widened in surprise.

She set the packages down on the top step.

"Please, Jesse. If you would just give him his birthday gifts."

She turned, walked back to her jeep, and slipped inside. There were no tears now, though. She was done with that. What she did have left was resolve. She was going to keep trying to talk to Jesse and keep trying to see Blake and talk to him. Even if Jesse thought that was never going to happen.

It *was* going to happen. She was going to get to know her son.

As she pulled away, she saw Jesse lean down and pick up the packages and carry them inside.

There was that, at least.

Unless, of course, he just dumped them in the trash when he got inside.

Jesse walked inside, staring at the packages in his arms. Blake's birthday. Just another thing he hadn't known. He found Blake sitting at the table in the kitchen.

"I heard her voice. My mo—Heather's." Blake looked up, that protective look he'd come to recognize firmly etched on the boy's face. "She... she didn't want to come in?"

"She just dropped by for a moment." He set the packages on the table, not feeling a bit guilty that he hadn't let her in. She didn't deserve to come in. To spend time with Blake. "She brought some cinnamon rolls. Her mother makes them at Sea Glass Cafe. They're good. Want one?"

"Sure, I'm starving."

Of course, he was. Jesse got out some plates, served up the cinnamon rolls, and then stared into the fridge. He had no milk. No orange juice. He turned to Blake. "Um... I've got nothing for you to drink, really."

"I'll take a soda if that's okay."

"Sure." Why not? But he was definitely going to have to get better food and drinks stocked up for as long as Blake was here.

And how long would that be?

He sat down across from Blake and glanced at the packages, renewed anger surging through him. He pushed the gifts toward Blake. "Heather brought these for you—" He stared at Blake. "She said today is your birthday."

Blake's eyes widened in surprise. "She remembered?"

He just nodded, trying hard to keep a scowl off his face, and took a bite of the roll.

Blake opened the gift bag and pulled out a t-shirt. And a pocketknife. He was a bit irritated that Heather was giving Blake presents. He hadn't even known today was his birthday. Of course, he hadn't known a single thing about his son until yesterday.

Then Blake unwrapped a small, flat box and pulled out a print. "What's this?" His brow creased as he stared at it.

Jesse glanced over. "Heather is an artist. She draws stuff. Illustrates."

"It's a blonde boy playing by the ocean. You think..." Blake paused and looked at Jesse. "You think that she thought of me and drew this? Kind of like what it would have been if—you know—things were different?"

"I honestly don't know, son."

Blake nodded and set down the print. "She signed it, too."

So now Blake could have a Heather Parker original, too. Just great. *Extra* special. He scowled in spite of his best intentions and turned his attention to the breakfast.

They finished their breakfast—such as it was with the unwelcome but very tasty cinnamon rolls—and Jesse took their plates to the sink. "So, I thought we'd do some shopping today.

Get some clothes and anything else you need. We can call them birthday presents. Or just... things I'd like you to have."

"I don't want to be any trouble. You don't have to buy me stuff."

"Oh, but I want to. I want to very much." Jesse crossed over and sat by Blake. "I wish there was something—*anything*—I could do to make up for missing so much of your life."

"But buying things won't change that."

Wise boy. "No, but it's something I want to do." Then he grinned. "And we need to get more food. Man, you can eat."

"I'm sorry. I try not to eat so much. It makes my aunt mad."

"You can eat as much as you want here. Doesn't make me mad. Glad to have someone to cook for."

"Mom always said she liked to cook for me, too. She was a really great cook. She always liked to make my favorite dinner for my birthday." Blake's eyes clouded, though he tried to hide his pain.

"She sounds like a really great mom."

"She was. We had the best time. Just the two of us. We had a great life until... well, the last year. It was hard. I missed a lot of school taking care of her. She tried hard to fight the cancer. I think she thought she was strong enough to will it away so she could stay with me." His voice cracked. "But... it was stronger than she was."

His heart broke just seeing the pain in Blake's eyes. Jesse reached over and touched his arm. "I'm so sorry. That must have been so hard."

He nodded. "I'm just missing her more today. She always made such a big deal out of my birthday."

And how could he compete with that? But surely he could do something to cheer the boy up.

Jesse looked at the clock. "I've got to call Leo. He's my second in command on The Destiny. My boat. I have a boat, a business. We do dinner cruises and sunrise cruises and people rent it out for parties and weddings and stuff like that."

"Wow." Blake's eyes widened. "Can we go see it?"

"Of course."

"I've never been on a boat. Well, a canoe once in adventure club with my school."

"Then we'll take a cruise on The Destiny. Want to go tonight?"

"Yes." Blake's eyes sparkled with excitement.

"A dinner birthday cruise it is." It wouldn't be as great as a special dinner made by his mother, but at least it would be some kind of celebration. He could at least do that much.

CHAPTER 19

J esse talked to Delbert, got the name of a lawyer, and put a call into her while Blake was getting ready for their shopping trip. He briefly explained the situation and they made an appointment for first thing tomorrow morning.

He and Blake headed into town, walking along the streets as he pointed out things along the way. "There's the town park on the harbor. And this whole walkway here is called Harbor Walk."

They headed to Magnolia Avenue and stopped at Beyond the Bay, a reasonably priced clothing shop. They bought a handful of shorts, some t-shirts, a pair of slacks, and one nicer shirt. Never know when that might come in handy. Then they bought a swimsuit and a new pair of shoes. Blake kept protesting it was too much, but Jesse couldn't help but feel it wasn't enough. Not nearly enough.

They walked out of the shop, each laden with bags. "You want to get some ice cream? Then I think we're going to have to drop off these packages and grab my car to go grocery shopping."

"I'd love some ice cream."

"Then we'll head to Parker's General Store. Best ice cream in the area."

"As in Heather Parker?" Blake asked.

Yes, much to his annoyance, everything seemed to be connected to Heather. Wasn't much he could do about that, though. "Heather's aunt runs the store, and Livy—you met her yesterday—she runs the cafe." He led the way down the street and they ducked into the general store.

Donna saw them, waved, and hurried over. "So, this must be Blake."

"Yes, ma'am." The boy said with every bit of formal politeness.

Donna's eyes filled with warmth and welcome. "I'm *so* glad to meet you."

"Blake, this is Donna." Jesse held up the

packages. "We've been doing some shopping. Now we've come for some ice cream."

"Ah, I see. Well, you've come to the right place. Here, I'll walk over into the cafe with you."

They headed through the opening from the store to the cafe, and Livy greeted them. "Hi. Did you get the cinnamon rolls?"

"We did, and they were so good." Blake nodded enthusiastically.

Evelyn walked out of the kitchen and froze, staring at Blake. "Oh... my." Her words drifted over to them and her hand reached up to her throat.

She slowly walked the distance over to them, her tear-filled eyes never leaving Blake, and held out her hand. "Blake, I'm—Evelyn."

Evelyn stood there, staring down at Blake's hand in hers. Her grandson's. The tsunami of emotions almost brought her to her knees. Grandson. Her grandson.

"She's your grandmother," Livy explained to Blake.

His eyes filled with hope and wonder. "My grandmother? Wow."

Evelyn smiled. "Wow, indeed. I'm so glad to get to meet you."

"Me, too. I mean, meet you. Wow, I have a lot of family here."

"That you do."

"We came for some ice cream," Jesse said as he dropped the packages he was holding on a chair at a nearby table.

"Sit, I'll get it for you." Evelyn could still not take her eyes off Blake.

"No, you sit with them, Evelyn. I'll get the order," Livy insisted.

She sat at the table across from Blake and Jesse. The boy's eyes were so like Jesse's, but she could see bits of Heather when he smiled. The little half-smile that Heather did.

"What flavor do you want, Blake? And a scoop of ice cream, a cone, or a shake?" Evelyn asked.

"Chocolate shake, please, ma'am. It's my favorite."

"You don't have to say ma'am to me. You can just call me... How about Evelyn?" She'd love to suggest Grams or Gramma or Grammy, but... things were moving so fast for the boy.

"Okay... Evelyn." Blake nodded.

They got their order and sat at the table. Conversation lagged. She wanted to ask so many questions but didn't want to make him uncomfortable.

Jesse broke the silence. "So, today is Blake's birthday."

"It is?" Shock swept through her. Of course he'd have a birthday, but today? She immediately wanted to buy him a gift. Something. How many birthdays had she missed?

"He's sixteen today."

Sixteen years ago her daughter had had a baby, all alone. Without any family around her for support. Guilt squeezed her heart for not being there for Heather.

"Heather gave me one of her signed drawings for my birthday," Blake said.

"Oh, that's a nice gift." She glanced at Jesse and he didn't seem thrilled. At all.

"And Jesse is taking me on The Destiny tonight."

"That will be fun. A birthday dinner cruise." She saw that Blake had finished his shake. "You want another one?"

"I... um, I'm kind of hungry."

"How about a sandwich?"

"Yes, ma'am—I mean Evelyn."

She got up and walked to the kitchen, pausing for a moment to lean against the counter. She was getting a sandwich for her grandson. A huge smile broke across her face. and she hurried to make him a big sandwich with a side of fruit and some chips. Then she grabbed a piece of peach pie. If it was up to her, she'd put some meat on that boy's bones.

Blake didn't disappoint. He ate every single bite.

Jesse laughed when Blake was finished. "I'm going to go stock up our fridge after this."

"You're welcome to come here and eat anytime. On the house, of course," Evelyn offered, hoping that she'd get to see a lot of Blake now.

"Is that okay, Jesse?" Blake turned to him.

Jesse laughed again. "Yes, that's fine. Evelyn is a much better cook than I am, even if I have learned a lot about cooking since buying The Destiny. Anyway, we should go. Still have the grocery shopping to do before heading over to The Destiny."

Evelyn heard the door to the cafe opened

and sucked in a quick breath when she saw her daughter enter.

Jesse caught her staring and swiveled to look at the doorway. His jaw clenched and he rose. "Time to go, Blake."

The boy rose. "Thanks for the shake and for the sandwich." He said politely to her before he turned to leave. Then he stopped with one hand still on the back of the chair he was carefully putting back in place.

Ah, he'd seen Heather.

CHAPTER 20

Heather paused as she came through the door of the cafe and her eyes adjusted from the bright light outside. Then she saw them. Her family at a table with Blake. Just like they were finishing a normal family meal.

Her family without her, of course.

Jesse knew she was here. She could tell because he stood with his shoulders squared and his jaw set in a firm line of anger. She took in a deep breath and crossed over to the table.

"We were just leaving." Jesse's words were as hard as concrete. Harder.

"We're getting groceries. I eat a lot." Blake gave her a tentative smile and a shrug.

"I just made him a sandwich," her mother

said as she rose, clearing up the plates on the table, a slightly guilty look on her face.

"I'm sorry I didn't pop in earlier." What else could she say? It was obvious that Jesse didn't want her here. Didn't want her anywhere near Blake.

"Yeah, that would have been nice," Blake said.

Jesse just clenched his jaw tighter.

"Jesse, can we talk?" She looked straight at those angry eyes.

"No." He turned. "Come on, Blake." He walked right past her toward the door.

"Um, bye," Blake said as he turned to leave.

She reached out and caught his arm. "Happy birthday."

"Thanks. And thanks for the birthday presents."

"You're welcome."

"I... uh... I should go." He glanced to where Jesse had already slipped out the door.

She nodded and watched as he hurried after Jesse.

She sank into a seat at the table. "Jesse is never going to talk to me."

Her mom set the plates back on the table

and sat down. "It will take time. He's very angry right now."

"I know." She stared at the empty shake glasses on the table, incredibly and ridiculously jealous of anyone who'd had a meal with Blake. Even her own mother.

"But it looked like Blake was glad to see you. His eyes lit up when you came in. I bet he wants to get to know you."

"If Jesse ever lets that happen." Disappointment swept through her. She stood. "Here, let me help you clear the table. And then I think I'm going to get me one of those magical shakes." Though she doubted that drowning her problems in chocolate was going to help much. But it couldn't hurt either.

Jesse and Blake headed to The Destiny after buying enough groceries to feed a football team. Or maybe feed just Blake for a couple of days. Jesse had made healthy choices. Fruit, milk, cereal that wasn't just all sugar, whole wheat bread, and organic peanut butter. That was all healthy, wasn't it? He'd also gotten steaks, chicken, bacon, and eggs. Though bacon wasn't really good for a person, but it sure tasted great.

At the end of the pier, he paused. The Jenkins twins were headed his way. He wasn't exactly sure how to deal with this. He didn't want to hide the fact that Blake was his son, but he didn't really want the twins to broadcast the news far and wide, either. He needed time to get adjusted to it all and most importantly talk to the lawyer tomorrow.

There was no escape, though. They were headed directly for them. He glanced quickly at Blake, hoping this didn't go badly...

"Well, Jesse Brown, there you are," one of the twins said.

"What happened?" He pointed to the other twin who was walking with a cane and had one of her ankles in a walking boot.

"I wasn't being careful, and I twisted my ankle. Have to wear this old thing for a few weeks."

"Jillian always has been a bit clumsy."

Ah, now he could tell them apart. At least for a few weeks.

"I am not clumsy. The step was uneven," Jillian insisted, then turned back to look at Blake. "And who is this?"

"This is Blake," Jesse said. Maybe that would be enough?

"Blake?" Jackie questioned, obviously wanting more.

"Yes, he wanted to see The Destiny, so I said I'd take him out on her tonight."

"Oh, that's nice." Jillian raised an eyebrow, obviously wanting to ask more questions.

But he wasn't going to let that happen. "Hey, we really have to run. Lots to do before we cast off. Hope your ankle gets better soon."

"Nice to meet you two," Blake said politely. Of course. His mother had raised him right.

He circled around the twins and strode toward The Destiny, wanting to put space between them and the twins before more questions came up. Though he was certain the twins would be asking everyone they saw who this Blake kid was.

Blake jogged to catch up with him and stopped just as they got to the gangway. "Jesse, do you not want anyone to know—you know— to know I'm your kid?"

Jesse's heart clenched. He'd messed this one up. "No, not at all. It's just…" How to explain it?

"It's okay, you know. I can just be some kid

169

you're showing around. You don't have to tell people." Blake looked down and scuffed his shoe.

Jesse reached out and took hold of Blake's shoulders. "No, I would like the whole world to know. I just want to talk to the lawyer and see if we can get some legal things settled. I don't want anyone stirring up trouble. And those Jenkins twins? Lovely ladies, but they like to...ah...gossip. A lot. And I just want to see where we stand legally before people start interfering."

Blake nodded. "Makes sense. And Jesse?"

"Yes?"

"I appreciate you helping me get emancipated. And letting me stay with you."

"It's the least I can do." And to tell the truth, he didn't want the boy to become emancipated... he wanted him to legally become his son. But whatever happened legally in all this mess, he was never going to lose contact with Blake. He was going to be in his life in whatever way he could. And with that thought firmly planted in his mind, he led his son onto The Destiny, determined to give him the best birthday possible.

CHAPTER 21

Jesse met with the lawyer early the next morning. She'd wanted to meet with him alone first, look through what paperwork he had from Blake, and find out everything he knew about the situation. Which wasn't much. She was going to take the paperwork and look into some details, and then she wanted to meet with Blake once she'd done that. He walked out of her office frustrated. At this point, he had no clue what would happen next. What could happen legally. The lawyer encouraged him to try and contact Blake's aunt again. She also said if she could track down what lawyer had handled the paperwork when Christina died, she would try to contact that firm, too.

He swung back by his cottage to pick up

Blake, and they headed to Sea Glass Cafe for a late breakfast. Blake asked a million questions about the lawyer visit, but unfortunately, Jesse didn't have any good answers for him.

"But I swear, I'm doing everything I can. We will work this out. I promise."

Blake looked skeptical. And who could blame him? He'd had a rough couple of years. But Jesse was determined that Blake's tough time was ending now.

They walked into the cafe and sat down, and Emily came over to their table. "Hey, you must be Blake. I'm Livy's daughter, Emily. So we're related in some kind of complicated way. Good to meet you."

"Nice to meet you," Blake said.

Emily slipped into the chair next to Blake. "So, you've been meeting the whole family, huh?"

"I think so..." He turned to Jesse. "Are there more?"

"There's Donna and Evelyn's mother, Patricia. But on my side of the family? I've got nothing for you, kid. I was an only child and my parents are gone."

"Oh, wait until you meet Grandmother Patricia. She's... interesting. And if you get the feeling she doesn't like you, don't worry about it. She doesn't really like anyone." Emily grinned.

"We're going to have breakfast, want to join us?" Jesse asked.

"Sure, I've got time."

They ordered breakfast with waffles, eggs, and bacon. Emily kept up a constant chatter about the cafe, Parker's, and the upcoming Harbor Festival.

"The festival is kind of neat. Lots of booths. Lots of food. Crafts. Art. And music. They usually have really great music."

"Sounds like fun."

"It's coming up next week. You should come."

"I'm not sure how long I'll be here." Blake shrugged and looked at Jesse.

"You can be here as long as you want, I hope. We just need to work out the legal logistics." He hoped he wasn't promising what he couldn't deliver.

Emily stood after they finished their meal. "Hey, I was going to go to the beach this afternoon. Wanna come? I love going shelling, and the weather is perfect today."

Blake looked at him. "Can I?"

"Of course." He'd wanted to take Blake

fishing, but that could wait. It would be good for him to have a friend his age.

"'K, I have to run home and put on my suit. I'll swing by Jesse's cottage and get you?"

"Sounds good." Blake nodded.

Emily swept out of the cafe.

"She's got a lot of energy," Blake said as he watched her leave.

Jesse laughed. "That she does. Good luck keeping up with her on your shelling adventure."

Emily hurried home and burst in the front door. "Mom, you home?"

"In the kitchen."

Emily entered the room. "Hey, I met Blake."

"You did?" Her mother paused from emptying the dishwasher, a plate in one hand and a cup in the other.

"Yeah, at the cafe. And I asked him if he wanted to go to the beach with me this afternoon."

"That was nice of you."

"Well, he doesn't know anyone here. I just thought he might like to hang out for a while.

Besides, it's kind of cool that I have a..." She shrugged. "Some kind of cousin."

"Second cousin, I think. But don't quote me on that."

"I never had a cousin, so I think it's great." Emily went off to change and called out as she was leaving. "Be home later."

She hurried over to Jesse's cottage and knocked. Blake answered. He was wearing swim trunks, a t-shirt, and a ball cap. She nodded in approval. "You ready?"

"All set."

Jesse came up behind him. "You guys have fun."

"We will." She held up her favorite teal mesh shelling bag. "Hoping for a good haul today."

They headed around the cottage to the beach and walked to the water's edge. "It must be nice to live here where you can go to the beach all the time," Blake said.

She shrugged. "I guess. I've never lived anywhere else. And I do love the beach. Oh, I should get Grams to take us out to Pelican Cay on the boat. It's so cool there. Lots more shells there than here."

"That would be fun. But like I said, I'm not sure how long I'll be here."

She paused. "That must be tough. Not knowing where you're going to be and what's going to happen."

"If Jesse can help me become emancipated, then I won't have to worry about other people controlling my life and where I live." Determination flashed across his features.

She couldn't imagine becoming emancipated. Not having her family to depend on. She couldn't imagine just finding her real parents. She was a bit in awe of Blake and all that he'd done to try and change his life and make it better. "I'm sure Jesse will help in any way he can. He's a nice guy. So, you live with your aunt now. That's what my mom said."

"Yeah, but she's on this long cruise with her new boyfriend. This is like the fourth boyfriend she's had since I moved in with her. He—" Blake sighed and glanced away. "He doesn't like me much."

"Then he's a jerk. I've only known you for, what? A couple of hours? And I think you're okay." She bumped into him playfully. "And I've always wanted a cousin. Now I got one. Mom said we're second cousins."

"Really? That's cool."

"Come on, let's look for shells. I like it when I can find some bigger ones that aren't chipped. Oh, or pink shells. I love pink shells."

They wandered along the shore, occasionally picking up a shell and rinsing it in the water. If she deemed it a keeper, it went into the bag. If not, they tossed it back into the sea.

After a while, they went up to sit under some palm trees for a break from the sun.

"So, you know my mother, Heather, huh?"

"Of course. She's my mom's best friend, along with being her cousin. They were born on the same day. Cool, huh?"

"What's she like?" His voice was nonchalant, but he wasn't fooling her. He was eager for details about her, and she couldn't blame him. It must be so strange to just meet your birth parents at sixteen.

She pursed her lips, thinking of how to describe Heather. "She's great. So talented. Have you seen her art? I just love it. And she's fun. She doesn't come to town very often. Except this last trip. She's been here awhile. Her father divorced her mom and Heather stayed to help out."

"So Evelyn just got divorced from... I guess my grandfather?"

"Darren, your grandfather, is a jerk. He left Evelyn for this young girl about our mothers' age. But then, he always was—I don't know— mean? He's very demanding, and he never thought Heather did anything right. She actually moved out when she was really young. Finished high school living with Grams. Then she moved away."

"I didn't know all that."

"And she wasn't close to her mom, either. Well, not until this last year. Evelyn was like a trophy wife to her husband."

"My grandfather."

"Right. And then he divorced her, took the house and all the money."

"Sounds like a creep."

"He is. But Evelyn has worked hard since they split. She ran this big grand opening event at Cabot Hotel."

"Oh, I saw that place. The big hotel on the harbor." Blake shifted, digging his heels into the sand.

"Right. And I put together the history alcove for the hotel. Delbert Hamilton—he owns the hotel—he hired me to do it after he heard that I worked at the history museum. He's a great guy. Anyway, she ran the event, and it was spectacular. Now she's the cook at Parker's Cafe. Only don't let my mom hear you call it that. It's really Sea Glass cafe, but the town usually just calls it Parker's Cafe."

Blake looked a bit dazed as he took in all the information she was throwing at him. "And Heather and Jesse? They dated?" Blake tossed a shell from hand to hand, still trying his best to look nonchalant, and still not fooling her.

She frowned, unsure how to answer. "I really don't think they did. I mean, they obviously slept together because—" She paused and pointed to him. "You know, you exist." She grinned. "But I think they were always just really good friends. Until a few years back, and then they weren't. I'm not sure of the whole story."

"That's more than anyone else has told me."

"Have you asked Jesse?"

"He doesn't really like to talk about Heather. He's really mad at her. I mean, I don't blame him since she kept me a secret from him all those years ago. I wonder why she did that?"

"I don't know. She was young when she had you. Only a couple of years older than I am now. And like I said, her father was a creep and she and her mother weren't close. Evelyn just let Darren roll right over her and did what he said. Never stood up to him. And from what I hear, it was just constant criticism of Heather while she was growing up." She glanced up as a pair of pelicans swooped by, then turned back to Blake. "I can't imagine. Because Mom and I are so close. And my grandmother helped my mom raise me. They are like my biggest supporters."

"My mom was great, too. We were close." His eyes clouded.

"I bet you miss her a lot."

"I do. It seems strange to live in this world without her. And living with my aunt has just been so different. She doesn't really like having me around, so I try to stay out of the house as much as possible. I haven't really made any friends there yet. Most of the kids have grown up there their whole lives and have their own little groups of friends. I tried out for the baseball team thinking I might make some friends, but I got cut. I wasn't surprised though. I hadn't played for two years. I quit my team when my mom got sick. I needed to be home more for her."

She couldn't imagine the life he'd had. So

different from hers. At least it sounded like he'd had a great mom adopt him. "But, so Jesse's cool, right?"

"Yeah, he's great. I hope I'm not causing him too much trouble. And I need to find a job if I'm staying here a bit. I need to get some money to pay him back for legal bills."

"I bet he's not expecting you to do that."

"But I want to."

"I'm sure we could use help at Parker's. Either in the general store or the cafe."

"Really?" His eyes lit up with relief and gratitude.

"Yep. I'll talk to my mom and grandmother when I get home." He was family now. Family helps family.

"Thanks, I'd appreciate it."

"Hey, what are cousins for?" She laughed and sprang to her feet. Enough serious talk. "Come on. I'll race you back to Jesse's."

Jesse sat before a spread of invoices for food and supplies for The Destiny, trying to get them sorted and paid. This was a part of business ownership that he hated.

He heard Blake come in.

"I'm back here."

Blake came into the kitchen and slumped into the chair across from him, glancing at the papers. "Bill paying time?"

"Yep. And I hate it."

"If I stay here awhile, I could help. I'm a whiz at math. I took care of all the bills for Mom the last few years." He shrugged. "But I guess we need to see what happens first."

Jesse nodded. The uncertainty of everything weighed heavily on him. He wished he had answers to give Blake. "So the lawyer called and wants us to get a paternity test. Said that will help. You okay with that?"

"Sure." He nodded.

"Then she wants to meet you and talk to you. I'll set that up."

"I'm sorry to be such trouble."

"You aren't causing trouble. And we'll get this sorted out," Jesse said. "So, did you have fun at the beach?"

"I did. Man, Emily sure likes to go shelling. She's really picky about which ones she keeps."

Jesse almost said that Heather was the very same way. But he didn't want to bring up her name. At all.

Blake picked up a paper and looked at it mindlessly. "So...about Heather. Are you guys friends? Or were you until finding out about me ruined it?"

"You didn't ruin anything," he quickly assured him. "And Heather and my relationship... Well, it's complicated." He couldn't explain it to himself, much less to someone else. Best friends. Slept together once. And now? He could barely look at her without rage overcoming him.

Blake looked at him, waiting for him to continue. But how did he explain what he and Heather have? Or *had*, because right now he didn't care if he never saw her again. "We were friends when we were kids. And when she'd come back to town to visit."

"Like when I was... uh... you know."

Jesse closed his eyes, and the memories of that night swam before him. "Yes, like that night. I did sleep with Heather, obviously. Mistake. Big mistake. Things were never the same."

Blake looked startled or... hurt?

He rushed to explain. "No, not that it was a mistake that you were born because of that night. I swear, I've never been happier about anything in my life. I'm thrilled you came and found me. So, maybe that night was the best thing that ever happened to me." In all his anger at Heather, he hadn't stopped to consider it that way. But it was. Because of that one night, he had this son sitting right here at his kitchen table.

"So... I was wondering..." Blake sat up straight, looked him right in the eye. "I'd—I'd like to get to know Heather... if that's okay with you. I know you're mad at her. But I might not get another chance if I have to go back to Kansas. Not like this. In the same town and everything."

He probably shouldn't be surprised at the request, and he shouldn't let his anger interfere. But Heather had given the boy up. She'd given away her chance. And yet... Blake still wanted to get to know her.

Blake's expression was tentative and hopeful. He couldn't deny the boy anything. "If you want to get to know Heather, I won't stand in your way."

"Thanks, Jesse. I just wanted to make sure you were okay with it. Because I really do appreciate all you're doing for me." Blake turned and headed to his bedroom.

Jesse sat staring at the pile of invoices, trying not to be... what? Jealous? Was he jealous that Blake wanted to get to know Heather?

He hated how complicated his life and his emotions were these days. Except for the one thing that had exploded into his life bringing unexpected blessings. His son.

CHAPTER 22

Donna sat out on the point with Evelyn that evening, sipping some chamomile tea. She and Evelyn had gotten closer in the last few months. Probably the closest they'd been since they were young girls. And she was grateful for that. When Evelyn was married to Darren, she hadn't seen her sister very often. And Darren had disapproved of her. It was obvious. He thought running the general store was silly. And he never wanted Evelyn to participate in any family get-togethers, so she gradually quit coming to most of them.

Evelyn set her teacup on the table between them and slipped off her shoes. "So, how is the wedding dress coming along? Livy told me you went to see Ruby over on Belle Island and she's doing the alterations."

"She is. I think it's going to work out perfectly. She said she'll have it finished next week."

"I'm so glad that worked out. And I have most things arranged for the wedding. The food. Servers. And the girls are going to help me decorate on the big day. It's all going to be so lovely. Oh, and I found these lanterns, and we're going to have them all around the edges of the pavilion."

She smiled at her sister, in awe of her event planning abilities. "I sure did well in the sister department. You plan weddings. You're a fabulous chef."

"I didn't do so bad in the sister department either. You took me in when Darren threw me out of the house. Gave me a job at the cafe. And then you gave me part ownership in it."

"Because you're a big part of why the cafe is so successful." She leaned back in her chair and gazed up at the stars tossed above them. "So... I almost hate to ask. Have you told Mother about Blake?"

Evelyn let out a long sigh. "No, I haven't. I need to. It's just... I don't want to hear her opinion. Though I do need to tell her before she finds out some other way. And I don't want her to find out in front of Heather in case she goes into one of her... well, you know how she is."

A laugh escaped her lips. "Yes, I do know how she is. And she probably will have choice words about it. I'm sorry. But you're right that it's better if she first learns about it without Heather being around. Heather is having a hard enough time as it is."

"I'll tell her after the festival. My mind and time are busy with festival plans and wedding plans. I must tell her before the wedding, though."

"That is if she even comes." Donna shook her head. She still hadn't heard one word from her mother. She'd considered calling her, but what was she going to say? It was way too late to move her wedding now, and her mother had made it clear that it aggravated her that Donna hadn't bent to her wishes. Things were always so difficult with her mother. It made her even more thankful for the close relationship she had with Olivia.

Evelyn picked up her tea again and took a sip. "She'll come. Mom is always a lot of talk.

Likes things her way. But she wouldn't miss her own daughter's wedding."

Donna wasn't so sure but liked her sister's unwavering support. "I guess we'll find out, huh?"

"I guess we will. But whatever happens, you're going to have a beautiful wedding and we're all going to have a wonderful time."

And Donna believed that. She really did. She couldn't wait for her wedding day.

CHAPTER 23

A few days later, Jesse headed over to The Destiny, trying to stay busy to keep his mind off fuming about Blake going to meet with Heather. He didn't blame the boy. Who wouldn't want to get to know their birth mother? But he still hadn't gotten his anger at Heather under control. He couldn't believe that she would have made such a monumental decision without talking to him. Blake was his son, too. He should have had a say. And there was no way he would have given the baby up for adoption.

He stopped in his tracks, pausing under a trio of palm trees, and frowned. Would he have considered giving the child up?

No, of course not.

Though... they'd been so young. And he'd been so overwhelmed with life then. College, two jobs. It had been a blur of studying and working and little sleep. He'd lived in a real dump. A studio apartment that he could barely afford in an area on the edge of town that a parent wouldn't really want to raise a child in if they had any choice.

He raked his hands through his hair.

All this because of that one night so many years ago...

As much as he tried to forget that night, he still remembered it so clearly. Heather had shown up on his doorstep, furious and... so hurt and vulnerable.

Rage had flowed through him at the sight of the clear handprint her father's slap had left on her cheek and the red marks on her shoulders where he grabbed her. Jesse had pulled her inside and wrapped his arms around her, feeling her shaking. When she finally calmed down... just a little bit... she told him what happened.

She'd gone to see her parents after visiting with Livy and her newborn. Her father raged about Livy being unmarried and having a child, called her a tramp. And Heather defended Livy, standing up to her father. A practice that anyone rarely engaged in. In return, her father had lashed out and slapped her. Her mother tried to interfere, but he turned on her, too. So Heather fled the house.

And she'd come to see him. The one person she could trust. At least until that night was over...

He remembered she'd placed her hand over her cheek as she told him the details. There were no tears because Heather didn't cry. But he could see how devastated she was behind her wall of anger. He could still feel the protective feelings that had swelled through him.

She'd paced the floor as she told him what happened and he let her, knowing that was what she needed right then. He'd always known what she needed, even when she didn't. She finally plopped down on the couch next to him and he wrapped her in his arms again, comforting her.

And then...

One thing had led to another...

He'd just wanted to make things better for her. Take away her pain. But when he woke up in the early morning hours with her sleeping peacefully beside him, he knew he had to let her go. He knew what *she* needed. He had to let her get away from Moonbeam and her father. Even if it was the hardest thing he'd ever done. Heather was like a bird, longing to soar. He wasn't going to do anything to hold her back. Even if it crushed his heart in the process.

And, if he really wanted to admit the truth, he'd wanted to let her go before she had a chance to say *she* was going to leave *him*.

He shoved the memories away. What had happened couldn't be undone. And it really didn't matter. Nothing mattered now except figuring out the legal mess with Blake.

Heather sat at a table at Sea Glass Cafe. She mindlessly sketched some mock-ups for a children's book she'd been asked to illustrate. A teddy bear appeared on her page. Then a rabbit. A small girl with a puppy. Anything to ignore the seconds ticking by. She'd looked at the clock on the wall at least twenty times in the last few minutes. She put down her pencil and rearranged the salt and pepper shakers, lined up the menus so they were exactly parallel to the edge of the table, and straightened the roll of silverware. She'd been shocked when Blake called her and wanted to meet. Even more surprised that Jesse let him.

She mindlessly stirred her straw in the tea sitting before her. Not that the tea needed stirring. The ice cubes swirled around in the cool, caramel-brown liquid.

The door to the cafe swung open, and she looked up. There he was. Blake. He was dressed just like any other teenager in loose shorts and a t-shirt, a pair of flip-flops on his feet. All his clothes looked new. He'd tanned up some in the days he'd been here. A small, tentative smile rested on his lips as he wove his way across the room and slid into the seat across from her.

"Hi," she said softly, the words hard to get out past the whirling emotions surging through her.

"Hey."

"I was glad you called."

He just nodded.

"Are you hungry? Want to order?"

"I'm always hungry." He picked up the menu.

Emily came over to take their order. "Hey, Blake. Heather."

"Hi." Blake smiled at Emily.

"I talked to Mom, and if you want to work here, we could start you on Monday morning."

"That sounds great." Blake's smile spread into a grin. "I'd love that."

She took their orders and headed to the kitchen.

Heather looked over at Blake, wondering if he needed money. "You're going to work here?"

"Yeah. I want to start paying Jesse back for his legal bills."

"You don't have to do that. I can pay them."

Blake's blue eyes glittered with surprise. "You'd do that?"

"Of course."

"But, I want to pay them." He shrugged.

She decided not to press the issue.

"I went and met the lawyer lady. She seems smart. And she had Jesse and I get a paternity test."

Heather raised an eyebrow. "She did?"

"Yeah, so there's no doubt. We should have the results back next week."

There was no doubt in her mind that Blake was Jesse's son. They shared some of the same mannerisms. Those same exact eyes. Blake reminded her so much of the young Jesse she'd hung out with all those years ago. She didn't need a paternity test to know that Jesse was Blake's father.

"And she got a message to my aunt, somehow. And got it in writing that it was okay that I could stay here. I don't think my aunt was very interested in cutting her cruise short and coming back to get me."

"Oh, that's great. At least legally that much is sorted out."

"Yeah, she'll be back in the states in a couple of weeks." Blake leaned back in his chair and picked up his drink, taking a sip before casually asking, "So, are you and Jesse ever going to work things out?"

Direct question. Good question. And one she didn't have an answer for. "I hope so, but I don't know. He feels betrayed and I don't blame him."

"He's pretty mad."

"I know. He won't talk to me now. Maybe in time."

"I hope so. I don't want to mess things up with you guys."

"Blake, none of this is your fault."

"That's what Jesse said, but I still feel like I'm causing a lot of trouble."

"You're not." She leaned forward. "I... I

don't even know how to say this... but..."

He looked at her expectantly.

She pushed forward. "I'm sorry. About all of this. About you losing your mom. She seemed like such a great woman when I met her. And losing your dad, too." She reached out and almost touched his hand. Almost. "I thought I was doing the right thing giving you up for adoption. I thought I was giving you the best life I could."

Blake stared at her hand, just inches from his, then looked up. "Emily said that your dad was kind of a jerk. Mean. Didn't think you ever did anything right. And that you didn't have your mom's support either."

She nodded.

"And you weren't that much older than I am when you had me. I can't imagine having a kid."

She knew all the excuses she'd had when she made the decision. But it didn't make it any easier.

"Are you sorry that you gave me away?"

And there it was. The big question. The one she had no answer for. She swallowed, and in a surge of courage, she covered his hand with her own. "I don't have a good answer for that. I did what I thought was right at the time. I had nothing to offer you. Well, except for love. I did love you so. But I wanted what was right for you, not what I wanted. I wanted you to have a normal life with parents who loved you and could provide for you and give you things I never could."

She paused, watching the emotions flicker across his face. She so wanted to reach out and touch his face. Hug him. Hold him.

"But I've missed you every single minute of every single day. I've had this huge hole in my heart that nothing could fill."

"My mom was really great. You did choose good."

"I'm glad to hear that."

"She was the best mom ever."

And as much as she loved hearing him say that, it stung a bit, in a ridiculous kind of way.

Blake bit his lower lip. "But... but I'm glad I came here and found you and Jesse."

"I am, too. So very glad."

She took her hand away from his as Emily brought their meals. They sat and talked, each asking the other questions about their lives. The whole meal passed as though they were in some kind of surreal alternate universe, like watching a movie of someone else's life.

They walked out into the sunshine after a three-hour lunch that she wished could last even longer. The Jenkins twins hurried up to them. Well, as fast as Jillian could walk with her cane. Heather had heard the town talk that Jillian had twisted her ankle. At least she could tell them apart for a while.

"Heather, dear. So good to see you." Jackie said. "I see you're here with Jesse's friend."

Heather looked from Blake to Jackie. Jesse's *friend*?

"Jesse and I ran into them near the marina the other day," Blake explained and shrugged slightly.

She sent him a questioning look, and he nodded as if he understood her question. She turned to the twins. "This is Blake, my... son."

To the twins' credit, they quickly hid their surprise. "Isn't that nice? It's great to have you here in town, Blake," Jillian said.

"Are you enjoying your visit?" Jackie asked with a warm, friendly smile.

Heather breathed a sigh of relief. The twins could carry town gossip like no one else, but when it came down to it, they were warm, caring people, and she was grateful for their acceptance of Blake with no questions.

"I am. Moonbeam is kind of a cool town."

"So you're here staying with Heather?" Jillian asked.

Okay, they wanted a little more info. Some questions were inevitable.

"No, I'm staying with my dad, Jesse."

Jackie's eyebrow rose, but she quickly hid it with a smile. "That's lovely. Jesse is a very nice man." She turned to Jillian. "We should get you inside the cafe and let you sit down. Don't want to overdo the walking on that bum foot of yours."

"Yes, we should. It was nice seeing you two. Blake, enjoy your stay," Jillian said.

"Yes, ma'am," Blake answered politely.

The twins went inside and Blake turned to her. "So... you told them who I am."

"I hope that was okay."

"I'm fine with it. When we ran into them before, Jesse didn't say who I was. That I was his son. He wanted some of the legal stuff to get settled first."

"Oh, I didn't know that. And..." She paused, taking in the mixture of hope and uncertainty on his face. "I want people to know you're my son. I'm proud to have you as my son. There'll be some talk, of course. It is a small town and suddenly you pop up out of nowhere at sixteen. But I'm okay with the talk if you are."

"I'm good. I don't care who knows. I'm just—"

She waited for him to continue.

"I'm just glad I was able to find you guys."

"I am, too. Very glad."

"So, I guess I'll see you around?" Blake stepped back, changing the subject.

"Of course." She'd love to see him every day. All day. But she was lucky that Jesse had given her this much time with him.

"You going to be at the festival Jesse keeps talking about?"

"I am. I'm showing some of my artwork at a booth there and I told Livy I'd help out at the cafe booth if they need it."

"Guess I'll see you there, then."

"Yes, you will." And she'd count the minutes until then. "Call me if you need anything."

He nodded, turned, and walked down the sidewalk. She watched until he turned the corner, and then she leaned back against the brick wall of the front of the cafe.

That had been the most remarkable three hours of her entire life.

CHAPTER 24

J esse looked up from mopping the upper level of the Destiny. It didn't really need it, but it kept him busy and helped him squash his thoughts, even if it didn't help him salve his anger. Blake stood at the top of the stairs watching him.

He straightened. "Hi."

Blake crossed over to him and leaned against the railing. "Hey."

"Did you have a nice visit?" The petty part of him wanted Blake to say no, but it had been over three hours, so he doubted he'd get his wish.

"I did. We talked a bunch. She seems... nice."

Nice. That's one way of putting it. He

forced a noncommittal look. "I'm glad you got a chance to get to know her." *Liar, liar, pants on fire.*

"She said she's going to be at the festival. I'll probably see her again there." He looked at Jesse with a tentative expression. "I hope that's okay."

"Of course it is. She's your mother. I wouldn't do anything to get in the way of you having a relationship with her." As opposed to, say, Heather keeping any knowledge of Blake's existence from *him*.

Ah, his anger was eating away at him. He was going to have to find a way to deal with it. Somehow.

"Oh, and hey, we saw those twin ladies again."

"You did?"

"Yeah, and Heather told them I was her son."

He dropped the mop. "She what?"

"She said I was her son. And I said I was staying here with you and that you were my dad. I hope that's okay." He looked a little worried.

"Of course," he quickly assured him. But he wasn't okay with it. Heather had no right to decide when the town found out about Blake.

And, of course, she'd made *that* decision without asking him either. The anger he'd just resolved to control surged through him again.

"So, can I help with tonight's dinner cruise?" Blake asked.

"Sure. That would be great. How about going to the galley and see if the cook needs some help? His assistant called in sick tonight."

"Okay." Blake turned and headed toward the steps, then turned back. "You sure you're okay with everything?"

"I'm fine." He picked up the mop and swabbed the deck again, getting angrier with each swipe of the mop. "Just fine. Perfect even," he lied to himself.

The next day Heather opened her door to an insistent knocking.

"Jesse." Maybe he was finally ready to talk. They needed to. She needed to explain.

But instead, he pushed past her, stalked into the condo, and whirled around to face her. "Who do you think you are?" His words came out in a rush of fury, almost knocking her over in their force.

"What do you mean?" She frowned.

"You decided, without asking me, I'd add —oh, but you never consult me about anything concerning Blake, do you? You decided to tell the twins—of all people—that Blake is our son."

"I—"

"What is wrong with you?" His steel-blue eyes blazed with indignation. "They spread gossip all around town. He doesn't deserve that."

"The town will find out soon enough. And I'm not ashamed of him or anything."

"I'm not either," he spit out. "But Blake doesn't deserve to be the center of gossip."

"The twins were actually very kind to him when they found out. Their hearts are in the right place, even if they do like their gossip."

"And you just decided it was your decision to make for all of us. Decided when everyone finds out about Blake. I wanted to get more legal things in place before anyone found out anything about him."

"If you would have told me that, then I would have known that's what you wanted." She pushed back. "If you'd talk to me. If you'd—"

"I don't have to talk to you or discuss

anything with you. If I had my way, you wouldn't even see Blake."

"Don't say that." Fear rushed through her at the thought. But if he helped Blake become emancipated, surely Blake could decide to still see her.

"I'm going to petition to become his guardian. And if things work out, I'm going to adopt him. That's my plan." His eyes flashed with determination.

She reached out to grab the back of the chair to steady herself from the force of his words and his gaze. "You're going to *adopt* him?"

"If I can work it out legally, yes. He'll be my son. Or maybe I won't have to adopt him. I don't know how that works since he *is* my son."

And what wasn't said still rang out loud and clear. Blake would be Jesse's son, not hers.

"So, I'd appreciate it if you don't interfere. If you don't make any decisions regarding Blake. He wants to see you—and I *hate* that—but I won't stop it. *But...* I mean it, Heather, stay out of everything to do with his life. You had your chance, and you threw it away." He stalked past her and whisked through the door, slamming it behind him.

She sank onto the chair, her hand at her

throat. That was one angry man. And a man determined to limit her influence in Blake's life. Panic surged through her. She'd just found Blake. Would Jesse make it impossible for her to have any kind of relationship with him? He said he wouldn't stop Blake from seeing her. But that kind of put Blake smack in the middle of Jesse's war with her.

She pulled out her cell phone and scrolled through her photos until she came to the one she'd taken of Jesse at Magic Cafe. That wonderful night before all this mess had happened. He looked relaxed with a lopsided grin on his lips, and his eyes twinkled. How she missed the warmth in those eyes instead of the fire and ice that flashed anytime he saw her now.

Disappointment laced with fear threaded through her. Would Jesse turn Blake against her? She had such a fragile relationship with Blake so far. Jesse said he wouldn't stop Blake from seeing her...but would he keep his word?

She'd never seen Jesse so angry in all the years she'd known him. And the thing was... she didn't blame him.

She clicked off her phone and rose from the chair. She sucked in a deep breath and pushed away her fear and self-pity. She resolved right then and there not to let the problems between her and Jesse stop her from getting to know her son. Nothing was going to stop that.

Not her past mistakes.

Not Jesse's anger.

Nothing.

CHAPTER 25

Donna looked up and smiled when she saw Barry coming through the screen door to the pool cage. He held a bottle of wine in one hand and a wrapped box in the other. He quickly crossed over and kissed her on the cheek before dropping into the chair beside her.

"I've missed you," he said as he set down the box and the wine bottle.

"You just saw me at Parker's this afternoon when you came in for ice cream."

"See, I told you it's been forever." He winked. "And I brought surprises. Would you like a glass of wine?"

"I'd love one. I just sat down and was thinking I should have brought out a glass to enjoy while I unwind."

"Then let me pop inside, open the wine, and grab glasses." He got up and disappeared inside.

She stared at the small package, wrapped precisely and finished off with a silver ribbon bow. Hm...

He returned, handed her a glass of wine, and grinned as he sat back down. "So, were you wondering what's in the box?"

She laughed. "Yes, I was."

"It's a little present I got for you. A kind of pre-wedding present. Open it."

She picked up the package and pulled at the ribbon. She lifted the lid and gasped. "Oh, Barry. It's just like Grace's." She pulled out a silver sand dollar on a delicate silver chain.

"After you told me about Grace's necklace and how much it meant to Grace and how Heather had given it to Blake... well, I thought that maybe you'd like one just like it. You said that Grace's husband gave it to her as a wedding gift... and I thought you might like the same for your wedding gift. I borrowed the original from Blake and had a jeweler cast this one for you."

She held it up and watched how the low lights surrounding them reflected on the necklace. "I love it. Just love it." She slipped it on her neck, and it came to rest below her throat.

"It looks nice on you," Barry said.

She reached up and touched the necklace. And somehow she felt even more connected to Grace Parker. Like she had Grace's blessing on this wedding. That they would be as happily married as Grace and her husband. "This was so thoughtful."

"Hey, I'm a thoughtful kind of guy," he joked.

"No, really. I don't know what I did to be lucky enough to have found you, and I can't wait to marry you."

"And I, you, the future Mrs. Richmond." His smile was warm and loving.

A rush of happiness flooded through her. She was getting married. To this wonderful man.

"I do have one question I've been meaning to ask, though." Barry cocked his head and stared at her.

"What's that?"

"You think the town will still refer to you as one of those Parker women after you become my wife?" His smile transformed into a chuckle.

She laughed again. "I'm certain they will.

Though I might become that Parker woman who married that Barry fellow."

"Ah, a longer title. Well, that works."

They settled back in their chairs as the stars flickered above them. She so enjoyed these quiet evenings with Barry. Soon, they'd have morning coffee, and meals, and still these quiet evenings.

"You almost packed up?" she asked him.

"I am, though I have the rental until the end of the month. I thought I'd bring over some of my things. I don't want to crowd you."

"You won't crowd me. I've been rattling around in this big old house all on my own for years, except for that brief time that Evelyn moved in. There's plenty of room."

"You worried at all about how... different it will be? We've both lived alone for a long time."

"I'm sure there'll be some adjustments, but I'm fine with that because in the end I'll be married to a man I adore."

"You always say the right thing, my love."

She reached up and touched the silver sand dollar that had warmed from resting on her skin. What a thoughtful and lovely gift. Just like Barry to think of something so special, so personal.

She glanced over, watching him stare out

over the water, watching the moonbeams dance across the ripples in the water. She wished she could just wrap this evening up in a pretty package—like her gift—and keep it forever.

He glanced over and took her hand in his. Maybe she didn't need the evening wrapped up after all. She would have him here with her every single day. And that was better than any present. How had she been this lucky to find a love like this? She didn't know, but she was very grateful. For Barry, for her family, for the life she had here in Moonbeam. Gratitude overwhelmed her as she squeezed his hand and he smiled. That special smile he gave only to her. The one that warmed her to her very core. Yes, she was one lucky woman, and she counted down the hours until their wedding.

CHAPTER 26

"Oh, shoot." Evelyn paused as she sorted out a tray of sandwiches at the Sea Glass Cafe booth at the festival.

Donna glanced over at her. "What's wrong. Did we forget something?"

"No, look. Incoming. It's Mother."

Donna looked up and frowned. "What's she doing here? She's not really a browse around a festival type person."

Patricia walked up to their booth. "Good morning, girls."

"Hi, Mom." Evelyn glanced over at Donna and shook her head slightly. She still hadn't spoken to their mom about Blake.

"What are you doing here?" Donna asked.

"Some of the ladies who are moving to the

new retirement place here in town wanted to see what the festival is all about." She nodded toward a group of ladies standing around a jewelry booth across the distance.

"Oh, that's Margery's booth. She makes the most interesting jewelry with silver and sea glass," Donna said.

Their mother shrugged. "I guess."

Evelyn tried not to roll her eyes at their mother's obvious lack of enthusiasm. Donna bumped against her and motioned her head to the side. Evelyn looked that direction and her mouth fell open. Blake was headed over to their booth with a wide smile on his face. Her heart double beat, and her pulse raced.

This was not good. Not good at all.

"So, don't you want to go join your friends?" Evelyn quickly asked her mother, hoping to send her off in the opposite direction and avoid any confrontation. She should have already told her mother about Blake.

"I will. I thought I might get a cup of coffee from you. You do have coffee, don't you?"

"Ah, sure." Evelyn hurried to pour a cup and handed it to her.

Blake stepped up to the booth. "Hey, Evelyn. Hi, Donna."

"Hmph," Patricia said with a disapproving look on her face. "Whatever became of children using the proper names for adults?"

"I..." Blake's eyes widened.

"We told him to call us by our first names. Blake works at Parker's." Evelyn took in a deep breath.

Emily came rushing up to the booth. "Oh, hey, Blake. Hi, Grandmother." She sent Donna and Evelyn a questioning look.

Evelyn stepped out of the booth and came around to Patricia. She had no choice. Now was the time. Any hopes of talking to her mother privately—and with Blake nowhere near—were gone.

"Mother, this is Blake. Blake, this is my mother, Patricia Beale." She paused and sucked in a strengthening breath and plunged on. "Mother, Blake is Heather's son."

Patricia gasped and clutched her cup of coffee. "Her what? Heather doesn't have a son."

Blake shifted from foot to foot, and Emily stepped close to him. "She does, Grandmother. And Jesse Brown is his father."

Patricia's features settled into a broad, disapproving frown. "I... I told you girls, I didn't want to have any scandal and gossip if I moved back to town. This just won't do."

"Mother," Evelyn said sharply.

"What?" Her mother's eyes widened with innocence.

"Blake is part of our family." She moved over to stand on the other side of him and placed her arm around his shoulders.

"Does... does everyone know?" Patricia whispered as her gaze swept the crowd.

"Quite a few people. It's not a secret." Though it surprised Evelyn that more people didn't know since Heather had said the Jenkins twins knew. But for once, they hadn't spread the news and left it up to the family to tell the town in their own time.

"I just—" Her mother looked Blake over carefully, scanning from his head to his feet, then shook her head. "This family never ceases to amaze me."

"I know, we were really excited, too." Evelyn was well aware what her mother really meant, but she refused to let her ruin things. "We're thrilled to have Blake here."

Evelyn sensed more than saw someone come up beside her.

"Grandmother." Heather stood at her side.

"Heather, what is this I hear?"

"I assume you heard about Blake, my son?"

Patricia shook her head. "I did. And I'm not pleased."

Heather took a step forward, her shoulders squared and her jaw set in defiance. "You're not *pleased*? I don't want to hear it. We're all very happy that Blake found us." She flung her arm wide. "Very. And I don't want anyone to say anything otherwise. Do you hear me?" Heather actually pointed her finger and shook it toward Patricia.

Blake's eyes widened, and he stared at Heather with a look of admiration.

"I've never been happier about anything." Heather's eyes blazed with fury and determination.

"I see." Patricia huffed and set her untouched coffee on the booth. "I should go catch up with my friends." And with that, she walked briskly away from them without ever saying a word to Blake or acknowledging him as a member of the family.

"Don't worry about Grandmother. She's like that. She'll get used to the idea. And for the record, she doesn't like me very much either." Emily grinned at Blake and shrugged.

"I seem to cause problems for everyone," Blake said softly.

"Nonsense. We couldn't be more thrilled to have you here and part of our family," Evelyn assured him.

"And we love having you work at Parker's," Donna added. "We're very happy that you came and found Heather and Jesse."

Heather stood before Blake and touched his arm. "Grandmother can be... difficult. We've all learned to live with it. She's not very accepting, and she can be a bit... cold. Please don't take it to heart."

Doubt clouded Blake's eyes, and he looked a bit overwhelmed. Evelyn sighed. Patricia Beale could do that to a person.

Emily grabbed his hand and tugged on it. "Come on. Enough of Grandmother. Let's go walk around and get some funnel cakes. And fish tacos. Oh, and ice cream. Can't forget the ice cream."

"You two have fun," Evelyn said as they walked away. She turned to Donna and Heather. "That was... not great."

"No, but very typical Patricia Beale," Donna sighed.

"But she doesn't get to hurt Blake's feelings.

I'll do anything to protect him from her. Anything." Heather glanced over to where Patricia had joined her friends.

"We all will, sweetie. We all will." Evelyn sighed and turned back to get the booth ready, picking up her mother's untouched coffee and dropping it into the trash. Disappointment in herself swept through her. She should have told her mother before this. Protected Blake and Heather from this. Just another time she'd failed as a mother and now as a grandmother, too.

Donna walked over and hugged her. "Quit beating yourself up. I see it in your eyes. Mother is difficult in the best of times."

She sent her sister a grateful smile. "But I wish—"

Donna held up a hand. "It will all be okay. I promise."

She just hoped her sister was right.

CHAPTER 27

Donna took a break from working the Sea Glass Cafe booth to walk around the festival with Barry. They mingled in the crowd and paused at the many booths, looking at the arts and crafts and sampling the array of foods.

"I'm glad you could take a bit of time off from working. The festival is a lot more fun with you on my arm. Besides, I miss you." Barry paused near a trio of palm trees for them to take in some shade.

"And yet, you saw me last night."

"And soon, I'll see you every night and every morning." He gave her a special look that made her go weak at the knees. Did he have any idea he did that to her?

Delbert Hamilton came walking up to them,

an ice cream cone in his hand and a broad smile on his face. "This is the best festival ever. I remember it from when I was a young boy. I can't believe the town has kept up the tradition after all these years."

"They have. And Harbor Festival is my favorite festival of the year. Oh, though, maybe the Christmas tree lighting is. That's always so magical." Donna pursed her lips. "But the Beach Festival with the sand building contest is fun, too."

Delbert laughed. "Moonbeam sure likes its festivals, doesn't it?"

"We do." Donna glanced across the crowd. "Oh, look. Isn't that your friend Cassandra Cabot?"

Delbert whirled around and searched the crowd. "It is," he said with a quick intake of his breath.

Donna waved when Cassandra looked in their direction.

The woman waved back and headed through the crowd toward them with an older gentleman by her side. Her face broke into a warm smile as she approached. "Hello there."

"Ah... hello, Cassandra." Delbert stood

there with a bit of a star-struck expression on his face.

Donna smothered a smile. She'd been right. There was something between these two.

"Uncle, I don't know if you remember him, but this is Delbert Hamilton. He used to come to The Cabot back when we were kids."

The man reached out and shook Delbert's hand. "Ah, the man who bought The Cabot."

"That, too." Cassandra's gentle laugh floated around them.

"I heard you've done fine things with the place."

"You should come by and take a look around. I tried to keep her as close as possible to the original design."

"We're actually staying there for a few days while my belongings are delivered to my new place. Cassandra here is going to help me get things all set up."

"Splendid. Well, I hope you enjoy your stay." Delbert seemed inordinately pleased to hear that Cassandra would be at the hotel for a few days.

Donna looked from Delbert to Cassandra and was certain she could feel an undercurrent going on between them.

Cassandra turned to her and Barry. "And let's see. Donna and Barry, right? I do believe I met you at The Cabot's grand opening. This is my uncle, Ted Cabot."

"Nice to meet you," Donna said.

"Pleasure is mine, my dear," Ted said as his eyes twinkled.

Barry reached out and shook Ted's hand. "Welcome to the festival."

"Uncle Ted is actually moving back to Moonbeam."

"Really?" Delbert asked, still staring at Cassandra.

"He's moving into a new retirement place that just opened. Sunrise Village."

"Oh, my mother is moving there, too. I hear it's very nice," Donna said. "You'll probably meet her. Her name is Patricia Beale."

Ted coughed, and his eyes grew large. "Patricia is moving to Sunrise Village?"

"Do you know her?"

"I do. Well, I did. It's been years and years. I assume her husband is moving there, too?"

"Ah... no. My father passed away a little while ago."

"I'm sorry for your loss."

She nodded at his condolences. "Mother

was living at a retirement place in Naples, but she and a handful of her friends got dissatisfied with how it was being run and decided to move here. She's going to move in soon. After next weekend," she explained.

"Donna and Barry are getting married next weekend," Delbert added.

"You are? Well congratulations," Ted said, his smile genuine.

"Yes, congratulations. That's wonderful," Cassandra added, then turned to Delbert. "So maybe we'll see you at the hotel? Are you here in Moonbeam for a while?" A hopeful look flickered across her face.

Donna looked back and forth between Cassandra and Delbert, amused by the electricity between them. She nudged Barry and tilted her head slightly toward the pair. He exchanged a knowing smile with her.

Delbert nodded. "Yes, I am. Until after the wedding."

"That's great. I hope we'll see you around then."

"How about I arrange a tour for you and your uncle? I'll show you all around."

"I'd love that, Delbert." Ted nodded enthusiastically.

"That would be wonderful," Cassandra said, all the while staring at Delbert.

Delbert, for his part, grinned like an adoring schoolboy infatuated with the most beautiful girl in class. "Perfect. I'll ring your room tomorrow and we'll set up plans."

Donna smothered a grin. Yes, there was definitely something going on between those two.

Cassandra tucked her hand in the crook of Ted's arm. "Well, we'll let you all get back to your festival. We were just getting ready to head back to the hotel."

Donna watched as Cassandra and Ted disappeared into the crowd. Or, more to the truth, she watched Delbert watch them and smothered yet another grin.

"Interesting that Ted knew my mother," Donna remarked.

"It is, isn't it? Small world here in Moonbeam," Barry said.

"It's not like she ever stayed at The Cabot or anything. But I guess they crossed paths sometime." Donna frowned. "But I don't remember him being here. I'm not sure I've ever met him before."

"He and his brother ran The Cabot until

Ted moved away suddenly and left his brother to manage the day-to-day business of the hotel," Delbert said. "I heard he was still involved on the financial side, though, and did everything he could to try and keep the hotel open."

"She's open now, and she's lovely," Barry said. "I'm so glad you were able to buy her and restore her."

"Me, too. Me, too." Once again Delbert stared off in the direction Cassandra had headed, and Donna bit her lip to keep from grinning.

CHAPTER 28

Only four more days to the wedding, and Donna couldn't wait. She and Barry went to The Cabot to wrap up some last-minute details. Delbert waved to them from across the room when they entered, and they hurried over to him.

"There you two are. I hear everything is in order for your wedding. Evelyn was just here. You just missed her."

"She's a wiz at planning events. I'm lucky she helped so much with the wedding. I never could have pulled it off so quickly without her. I'm sure it's all going to be lovely and go off with a hitch."

"And I already have her booked to plan a big Christmas bash this holiday season here at

The Cabot. She's going to be in charge of decorating the hotel, too," Delbert said as he set a file down on the reception desk.

"I don't know how she finds time to do everything she does. These events and then being the chef at the cafe. She seems happy though." Actually, her sister amazed her these days. All that she did. What she'd accomplished. How far she'd come since hearing that her husband was divorcing her.

"She does. She's a lovely lady," Delbert agreed. "So I meant to tell you. I had RSVP'd to your wedding invitation thinking I was going to bring this woman I date sometimes socially. But that didn't work out. It will just be me."

Donna smiled, a plan hatching quickly in her mind. "Why don't you ask Cassandra if she'd like to come with you? She might enjoy seeing a wedding at the hotel after all this time."

Del's eyes lit up at her suggestion. "Well... maybe I could do that."

"It's a great idea." Barry nodded. "Ask her."

"And why don't you see if her uncle wants to come, too. I'd hate for him to just sit alone in his room. We'd love to have both of them, wouldn't we, Barry?"

"Of course."

"I'll ask her then. You're right, she might enjoy seeing a wedding here at the hotel. It's been a long time since there's been one here. I'm hoping to hire someone as a wedding planner for the hotel so we can have many more in the future." He grinned. "And don't worry, I know I can't steal Evelyn away from you, as much as I'd love to."

Just then Cassandra and Ted came walking through the lobby. Donna waved them over. "Perfect timing."

Cassandra greeted them with a warm, friendly smile. "We've just been to see Uncle Ted's new suite at Sunrise Village. He has a penthouse room with a view of the harbor. It's just lovely."

"I think it will work out perfectly. A two-bedroom with a small office. And a nice kitchen, not that I cook much." Ted grinned. "I'm hoping their dining room has good food, but I know there are lots of wonderful places to eat here in Moonbeam."

"I'm not sure where Mother's room is at Sunrise Village. She's been a bit quiet on the details. She hired a company to move her things and set up her place. We offered to help after the wedding, but—" She stopped, not wanted to air more family business. "I'm sure it will all work out fine for her."

She looked at Del and nodded, encouraging him to ask Cassandra.

Delbert stepped up next to Cassandra. "Could I speak to you for a moment?"

"Of course," Cassandra answered.

The two of them stepped away.

Ted nodded his head toward them. "I might just be the old uncle, but... those two seem awfully friendly."

Okay, so maybe Ted wasn't as oblivious as she'd thought. "I think so. I guess they were friends way back when Delbert would come here with his grandparents."

"That's what Cassie said."

Delbert and Cassandra walked back over to them. "Uncle, Delbert has asked me to Donna and Barry's wedding."

"Splendid. A wedding here at The Cabot again." Ted's enthusiasm rang out.

"Won't you please come, too?" Donna asked. "We'd love to have you. It just seems fitting for the first wedding here at the hotel after all this time."

Lines from laughter and life experiences deepened and lent even more warmth and friendliness to Ted's smile. "I'd be honored. I'd love to come."

"Great, it's all settled then," Barry said.

Delbert had a silly, befuddled, and bemused look on his face that was so in contrast to his usual all-business expression. Donna hid a smile. Maybe Cassandra would be coming around Moonbeam more now that her uncle was moving here. And maybe Delbert and Cassandra would be seeing more of each other.

She laughed silently at herself. She was such a hopeless romantic.

CHAPTER 29

J esse stood by the back window of his cottage, staring out at nothing, the piece of paper clenched tightly in his hand. The paper that confirmed what he already knew, right there on the page. Blake was his son. His thoughts bounced around in his head from one thing to the next. Blake. This was more than he'd ever hoped for, more than he ever knew he wanted. Ever knew he needed. A son.

He wasn't a man to cry, but he did have to blink rapidly to keep back the tears that threatened the corners of his eyes. The official confirmation just sealed the joy that flooded through him.

"Jesse?" Blake called out as he entered the cottage after a morning shift at the cafe.

His son was getting so entrenched here in Moonbeam, and he liked that. He needed to get all the legalities worked out. That is if Blake's aunt would ever get back in the country and respond to his lawyer. His life had changed so quickly and so much for the better.

"I'm back here." He stared down at the paper in his hands.

Blake walked up to where he was standing. "Hey, I made great tips today." His voice was filled with excitement. "I'm getting better at the job, too. I didn't mess up even one order today. Emily worked a shift with me, too. I really like working there at Parker's."

"Sounds like you're going to have some money to put into savings."

"I want to use it to pay for the legal bills," Blake insisted.

"That's not necessary," he insisted right back. He reached out and handed Blake the paper. "You should see this."

Blake scanned it and broke into a wide grin. "So this is proof. Though I just knew you were my dad as soon as I saw you. But this will help, right?"

"I hope so. I sure hope so. Because... I know you wanted to become emancipated...

but what I'd like to do is become your guardian... and then..." He paused and drew in a deep breath of air. "And then adopt you... become your legal father... if that's okay with you."

"Adopt me?" Blake's eyes widened. "Like *really* become my father?"

"Like really become your father. Legally become your father. Because I *am* your father."

"Wow."

"Wow, indeed. I'd like nothing more."

"I wanted to become emancipated so my aunt couldn't put me in the foster care system... but this would sure beat that." He grinned. "And we'd live here at your cottage?"

"We would."

"And I'd go to school here? At Emily's school, right? Moonbeam High School?"

"You would. I'm sure Emily would show you the ropes. Introduce you to more kids."

"Wow." Blake grinned again.

He wondered how many wows Blake could manage today. "So, the lawyer is going to work toward that, if you're good with it."

"I'm great with it." Blake frowned slightly. "Does Heather know you're doing this?"

"Kinda." But why should he give her all the

details? Heather hadn't even bothered to tell him the tiny little detail that Blake existed.

"I wish—" Blake stopped and shook his head.

"You wish what? You can tell me."

"I wish you and Heather could work things out. Get along together."

As much as he longed to give Blake everything he wanted, he didn't want to lie to him. "I'm not sure that's ever going to happen."

"You know, she was only a little older than I am now when she had me. I bet she must have been scared. She was all alone."

He paused and considered Blake's words. She probably had been scared. She certainly couldn't have turned to her parents for help. But she *could* have turned to him. Yet the realization of how frightened Heather must have been at the time was *possibly* beginning to chip away at the anger he'd been holding on so tightly to. *Possibly.*

"Can't you at least *try*?" Blake's eyes implored him.

And he'd *try* to do anything Blake asked of him. Anything to make him happy. "All I can do is promise to try."

Blake nodded. "Thank you." He turned and

headed to his room but paused and turned back. "It means a lot to me. I hope you two can work out your differences."

Differences. Well, that was one way to put it...

CHAPTER 30

Donna and Evelyn stood in a suite at The Cabot that Delbert had given them to get ready for the wedding. Donna insisted it was too much, but Delbert had insisted it wasn't. He won the argument. And it was nice to not have to travel in her dress. She just had to walk down to the pavilion.

"Ruby did a fabulous job with Grace's dress, didn't she? You look just lovely." Evelyn buttoned the top button and smoothed out a bit of lace.

"She did do a good job. I feel like I have Grace right here with us." Donna spun slowly in front of the full-length mirror. "It's simple and perfect. Just a tiny bit of lace. Not too frilly or anything."

"It is lovely to have the history of the dress, isn't it?" Evelyn handed her the bouquet. "Here you go."

"The flowers turned out lovely, Evie. I can't thank you enough for all your help with this wedding. I never could have pulled this off without you."

"Oh, you know me. I love planning events. And I can't think of a more rewarding event than my sister's wedding."

"So... do you think Mother is coming?" Donna frowned slightly. She hadn't heard a word from her since the Harbor Festival.

"I really don't know. I called and left two messages. She never called back. I can't imagine she'd miss it, but you know how stubborn Mother can be. Don't let her dampen your joy."

"I won't." She sighed. "I just sometimes wish we had a bit more—I don't know—*normal* parents?"

"Enough talk about Mother. She'll be here or not. But everyone else who loves you will be here. That's what counts." Evelyn gave her one more perusal from head to toe. "Yes, you look perfect. Are you ready?"

"I am. I'm so ready." The two sisters headed out to the pavilion, and Olivia joined them.

"Mom, you look beautiful." Her daughter's eyes shone with approval.

"Thank you."

"We've got everything set. I just have to signal them to start the music. Whenever you're ready. Oh, and Heather and Emily are sitting down in the front row."

"Perfect. I'm ready." Her heart skipped a beat as she glanced at the pavilion filled with friends and family.

The music started to play, and she walked down the sidewalk to the entryway to the pavilion. All the guests rose when they saw her, but she only had eyes for Barry, standing by the arbor, looking so handsome in a smart-looking suit. And if she didn't know better, she'd swear there were hints of tears at the corners of his eyes.

Olivia slowly made her way down the aisle.

"Come on, I'm ready to give you away." Evelyn grinned and took her arm.

Donna touched the silver sand dollar necklace draped around her neck then walked down the aisle on Evelyn's arm until they reached the front of the pavilion. The majestic view of the harbor stretched out before them with the last of the day's sunlight twinkling across the water like sparkling diamonds.

Barry reached out his hand and took hers, pulling her close to his side. He leaned close and whispered, "You look beautiful."

Her heart swelled with joy as she smiled up at him. They said their vows and before she knew it, she was Donna Richmond.

Barry kissed her gently and whispered to her, "I love you so, Mrs. Richmond."

"I love you, too," she whispered back, sure there had never been a happier moment in her life.

They held hands and walked back down the aisle. Together. As husband and wife. Or as the Parker woman who married that Barry fellow. Or just as a very, very happy couple.

CHAPTER 31

Heather left Livy standing with Austin —honestly, they were the *cutest* couple— and circled over to where Aunt Donna and Barry were sipping on glasses of champagne. "Hey, Donna. I don't know if you saw her, but Grandmother was here. She was in the last row at the far end. I guess she didn't want to miss her own daughter's wedding."

Donna scanned the crowd. "I don't see her."

"I don't think she left." At least she didn't *think* she had, but knowing her grandmother, who knows. "I could go find her if you'd like."

"No, that's okay. She'll find me if she wants to." Donna smiled up at Barry, and Heather grinned. Her aunt looked absolutely besotted. And that wasn't such a bad thing.

Delbert, Cassandra, and her uncle walked up to them. "Lovely wedding, Donna." Delbert kissed Donna's cheek.

"It was magnificent. I was so pleased to see a wedding here at The Cabot again. I wish much happiness to both of you." Ted Cabot shook Barry's hand.

"You look lovely, Donna," Cassandra added.

Heather looked across the crowd and leaned close to Donna. "Grandmother is headed this way."

Donna looked up quickly, and Heather could feel her stiffen beside her. Patricia Beale glided up to them in the way only Patricia could. "Donna," she said.

"Grandmother, I'm so glad you made it. And let me introduce you to Cassandra and Ted Cabot." She stood staunchly at Donna's side, uncertain if Patricia would say something... unexpected. But her grandmother wasn't focused on Donna anymore.

Patricia's face drained of color as she swiveled to see Ted and Cassandra.

"Oh." Patricia wobbled a bit on her high heels.

"Patricia, so good to see you after all these

years." Ted's eyebrows rose. He shifted his tie, then extended his hand toward her.

Patricia stared down at his hand but didn't take it.

Strange.

Ted pulled his hand back, and his smile dimmed slightly.

Patricia seemed to recover her poise. "Well, I just wanted to say—congratulations—I really must go."

"I'm glad you came, Mother."

Patricia just nodded and then—if Heather didn't know better because Patricia Beale never hurried more than her elegant gliding walk —she *sped* away from them and disappeared into the crowd.

"Sorry," Donna said. "Mother can be a bit —" She shrugged.

Ted stood staring after where Patricia had vanished. He finally looked back at them and smiled. "Ah, yes. Patricia is one of a kind."

Well, that's one way to describe Grandmother... A rather charitable way at that.

"Come, Cassandra, let's walk around a bit. I want to head over to the edge of the pavilion and watch the sunset. Delbert, that okay with you?"

"Yes. I'll grab us some champagne and we'll watch the sunset."

Cassandra took Ted's arm and the three of them headed over to the view at the end of the pavilion.

Heather looked across the crowd and saw Jesse standing with Blake. Her heart did a quick double beat at seeing the two of them standing together. Father and son. A sight she'd never imagined she'd see. And yet... there they were.

"If you'll excuse me..." She smiled at Donna and Barry and started to thread her way through the crowd toward Jesse and Blake, determination soaring through her.

Jesse watched as Blake headed over to talk with Emily. He was glad Emily was introducing Blake to a bunch of kids his own age. It seemed his son was easily slipping into life here in Moonbeam, and that pleased him. It pleased him a lot. All he wanted was his son to be happy. To have a good life. The best he could give him.

"Hi."

He whirled around at the sound of Heather's voice, his fists balling tightly until he forced himself to uncurl his fingers. He hated this automatic reaction he now had to hearing Heather's voice.

"I see Blake is off with Emily." Heather nodded in the direction the kids had headed. "Do you think we could talk?"

"Now's not a good time." He started to turn away, to avoid her—anything to avoid her—but she caught his arm.

"It's never a good time, is it?" Her eyes flashed, demanding he stop and listen. "But we need to talk. For Blake's sake."

"Don't even use that line with me. For *Blake's* sake. Right." His eyes narrowed.

"Yes, for Blake's sake. I've only ever done what I thought was best for him."

"Like giving him away?" He gritted his teeth, hating the icy-hot rage that swept through him every time he thought of Heather giving Blake up for adoption. Without one word to him. None.

"Like giving him to a woman and a man who could give him a normal, wonderful life. They were so in love. So happy. They had a nice home in a nice neighborhood. Just so... normal. What could I have given him?"

"A chance to grow up with his father?" He

tossed the words at her.

She paused and stared at him. Stared at him hard. "*My* father would have made living here in Moonbeam impossible, you know that."

He frowned—reluctantly. She was right there. Darren Carlson would have never helped his daughter and would have insisted she leave town. He wouldn't have wanted the embarrassment of an unwed daughter having a child.

"And Mom and I weren't on good terms then either. What did I know about being a parent? Nothing at all. I just wanted to protect Blake from my father and from a life of people talking about him in a small town like Moonbeam. I wanted him to have a wonderful, normal childhood. Not like mine."

He raked his fingers through his hair in exasperation. "But... you didn't tell me, Heather. How could you keep that from me?"

She didn't back down from his gaze. "Jesse, you were in school and working how many jobs trying to save money? Neither one of us had any way to support him." She glanced away, out to the harbor, before looking back at him. "And... well, you said it was all a mistake. That night we slept together. A *mistake*."

The pain was plainly etched on her face. Seared in the depths of her sapphire blue eyes. And it shocked him to his very core.

"But... I thought that was what you wanted. To be free to go back to your life. Not tied down here in Moonbeam." And he hadn't meant it anyway. He hadn't thought it was a mistake. He'd thought it was the best thing that had ever happened between them. But she'd looked so scared the next morning. Like she wanted to run. So he'd given her that freedom with his words.

She continued to stare directly at him, not letting him turn away from her pain. "I wouldn't have slept with you if all I wanted was to leave..." she said softly.

That hit him like a punch in the gut. It stung. And now that he was older, he was aware of the truth of her statement. She wouldn't have just casually slept with him. But back then, when they were young... when he was young and oh so very, very foolish.

Emotions smashed through him. The choices he'd made had led them to this point, too. He was as much to blame as Heather.

Her voice quieted, and her eyes filled with sadness. "I didn't want you to take on any responsibility or stay with me because of the baby. You made it clear you thought it was a mistake—it was *wrong*. So I didn't want to come crawling back asking for help. I wanted you to have your school, and your dreams, and your freedom. And I just felt so alone. Like I had no one to turn to for help. I was so... so scared when I found out I was pregnant."

"Ah... Heather." Guilt smashed through him. Why hadn't he just told her the truth back then... that he loved her? And he had. Probably since somewhere back when they'd first become friends. Though the words had never been said. If only he'd been truthful. The if-onlys flooded through him, crashed over him, mocked him.

"*I* didn't think it was a mistake." Her eyes flashed in defiance. "*I* thought that one night was so very right. I felt like all our years of being friends had fallen into place that night. That I was where I was supposed to be. But I woke up, and you were so sure that it *wasn't*. That it had been a mistake." She looked right at him. *Into* him. "You crushed my heart with those words."

And with her words right here, she crushed *his* heart. "Heather... I..." He reached out and took her hands in his. "I'm so, so sorry. I've been blaming all of this on you. But if I would have told you the truth all those years ago, everything would have turned out differently. You could have to come to me. We could have made the decision together." The enormity of his role in this whole mess crashed down on him. He'd been so cruel, so hard the last few weeks. Unwilling to listen to her to consider what she'd gone through. Unwilling to look past his anger. Embarrassment strangled him as he realized he'd made it all about him

Sadness lingered in her eyes. "We might have chosen to keep our son and tried to give him the life he deserved. Or maybe we still would have given him up for adoption. But you would have had a say in it." Her voice cracked as she said the words. "So... do you forgive me?"

"I do," he said, his own voice cracking with emotion. "I realize now that you did what you thought was best. What you thought you had to do. And I hope you'll forgive me for saying sleeping with you was a mistake."

"Because that one night brought us the best thing we could ever hope for, didn't it? It gave us Blake." There was an intensity in her eyes that he'd rarely seen.

He squeezed her hands. "That it did." He

released her hands and swept a lock of hair away from her face. "And, Heather?"

"Um?"

"I should have told you this years ago."

"What's that?" She searched his face.

"I should have told you..." He touched her cheek, and she smiled. "I should have told you that I love you. I have for... well... for forever. Since we were kids and best buddies. You have always been the only one for me."

Her eyes widened and she let out a tiny gasp. "What did you say?"

"You heard me." he grinned. "I said that I love you."

"I thought that's what you said, but I wanted to be certain." She cocked her head to the side and a delighted grin spread across her lips. "That's a very, very good thing to say to me."

"It is?"

"Yes, it is. Because I love you, too, Jesse Brown. Always have, always will."

He tugged her into his arms and kissed her. Right there where anyone and everyone could see. Because Heather Parker loved Jesse Brown. He didn't think he'd ever heard a better piece of news.

EPILOGUE

The Parker women sat out on the point at Donna's house, enjoying a pleasant summer evening. Barry was out of town on business and Aunt Donna had taken the opportunity to have all of them over for drinks and watching the sunset.

Heather leaned back in the chair, enjoying the company. She hadn't stayed this long in Moonbeam since she'd left right after high school, and to her surprise, she was loving every minute of it. At least since she'd started working things out with Jesse.

"So, how goes the legal process with Blake?" Donna asked.

"It's actually going better than we'd hoped. Blake's aunt has no real desire to be his guardian, and Jesse got temporary guardianship. It will take a while to get everything sorted out."

"And Jesse got Blake enrolled in school with Emily," Livy added. "They start in a few weeks."

"It's so cool to have my cousin at my school." Emily popped up from her chair. "I've been introducing him to all my friends. But Jeanie Francis has a crush on him, and she's way not good enough for him."

Heather laughed. "So, you're Blake's protector now, huh?"

"Hey, what's a cousin for?" Emily paced a few steps, then sank back onto her chair with a grin.

"Yes, whatever *is* a cousin for?" Livy teased.

"A cousin is to knock some sense into someone. To insist they keep trying to make things right." Heather smiled at Livy, glad for her cousin's insistence that she keep trying to get Jesse to listen to her. They had a tentative truce going now. No, better than that. He'd said he loved her. She wasn't sure where it would go from there, but for now, she was grateful for what she had. And she'd forever be grateful that Blake had come to Moonbeam searching for them.

"I'm so glad that you and Jesse are working things out," Evelyn said. "He's such a nice young man."

"He is, Mom. He is," Heather agreed.

"And things are going well between you and Austin?" Donna asked Livy.

"They are. He's up visiting his family right now, but he'll be back soon. He asked me to go with him, but things have been so busy at the cafe. I told him I'd go with him next time."

"Things are going pretty well for all of us, aren't they?" Donna raised her glass. "To the strength and resilience of the Parker women."

Heather clinked her glass with all of them. Yet another Parker women toast. There was just something wonderful about being a Parker woman. Something magical. She was just sorry it had taken her so long to figure that out. "To the Parker women."

Dear Reader,

I hope you enjoyed Heather's story. In the next book, **The Parker Family Secret**, there are more surprising secrets from the Parker women's pasts to be discovered.

Heather and Jesse continue to find their way with Blake.

And Patricia? She's still demanding and judgmental and... well, you'll want to read the next book and find out what all happens in Moonbeam.

https://kaycorrell.com/the-parker-family-secret/

As always, thank you so much for reading my books. I hope you're enjoying them!

Until next time,

Kay

AUTHOR'S NOTE

I hope you're enjoying the Moonbeam Bay series. I'm sure having a great time writing it. It's fun to have characters from other series pop in from time to time, isn't it? Just wait until you see what Camille is up to at the end of this series! Will it finally be the end of her troublemaking?

Or not…

I just wanted you to know how much I appreciate each and every one of you!

Kay

COMFORT CROSSING ~ THE SERIES

The Shop on Main - Book One

The Memory Box - Book Two

The Christmas Cottage - A Holiday Novella (Book 2.5)

The Letter - Book Three

The Christmas Scarf - A Holiday Novella (Book 3.5)

The Magnolia Cafe - Book Four

The Unexpected Wedding - Book Five

The Wedding in the Grove (crossover short story between series - Josephine and Paul from The Letter.)

LIGHTHOUSE POINT ~ THE SERIES

Wish Upon a Shell - Book One

Wedding on the Beach - Book Two

Love at the Lighthouse - Book Three

Cottage near the Point - Book Four

Return to the Island - Book Five

Bungalow by the Bay - Book Six

CHARMING INN ~ Return to Lighthouse Point

(This is a spin-off series from Lighthouse Point with cross-over characters. Either series can be read first.)

One Simple Wish - Book One

Two of a Kind - Book Two

Three Little Things - Book Three

Four Short Weeks - Book Four

Five Years or So - Book Five

Six Hours Away - Book Six

Charming Christmas - Book Seven

SWEET RIVER ~ THE SERIES

(This series is set in a fictional Colorado town of Sweet River Falls.)

A Dream to Believe in - Book One

A Memory to Cherish - Book Two

A Song to Remember - Book Three

A Time to Forgive - Book Four

A Summer of Secrets - Book Five

A Moment in the Moonlight - Book Six

MOONBEAM BAY ~ THE SERIES (2021)

(The charming town of Moonbeam is just over the bay from Lighthouse Point.)

The Parker Women - Book One (Jan 2021)

The Parker Cafe - Book Two (Feb 2021)

A Heather Parker Original - Book Three

The Parker Family Secret - Book Four

Grace Parker's Peach Pie - Book Five

The Perks of Being a Parker - Book Six

INDIGO BAY

Save by getting Kay's complete collection of stories previously published separately in the multi-author Indigo Bay series. The three stories are all interconnected.

Sweet Days by the Bay

Or buy them separately:

Sweet Sunrise - Book Three

ABOUT THE AUTHOR

Kay writes sweet, heartwarming stories that are a cross between women's fiction and contemporary romance. She is known for her charming small towns, quirky townsfolk, and enduring strong friendships between the women in her books.

Kay lives in the Midwest of the U.S. and can often be found out and about with her camera, taking a myriad of photographs which she likes to incorporate into her book covers. When not lost in her writing or photography, she can be found spending time with her ever-supportive husband, knitting, or playing with her puppies —two cavaliers and one naughty but adorable Australian shepherd. Kay and her husband also love to travel. When it comes to vacation time, she is torn between a nice trip to the beach or the mountains—but the mountains only get considered in the summer—she swears she's allergic to snow.

Learn more about Kay and her books at kaycorrell.com

While you're there, sign up for her newsletter to hear about new releases, sales, and giveaways.

WHERE TO FIND ME:

kaycorrell.com
authorcontact@kaycorrell.com

Would you like to join my Facebook Reader Group? We have lots of fun. We chat and they help me name characters or places. They see my covers before release. If you us, you'll also hear about sales and new releases first!

www.facebook.com/groups/KayCorrell/

I love to hear from my readers. Who is your favorite character? What series is your favorite? Feel free to contact me at
authorcontact@kaycorrell.com

Links to social media on next page.

facebook.com/KayCorrellAuthor

instagram.com/kaycorrell

pinterest.com/kaycorrellauthor

amazon.com/author/kaycorrell

bookbub.com/authors/kay-correll

Heather Parker has stayed home in Moonbeam longer than she ever thought possible. Which makes it really hard to keep avoiding Jesse...

Eventually they come to a mutual truce.

... and then a bit more.

But a surprise from the past threatens everything. Secrets come tumbling out and everyone is shocked by what Heather has hidden from them. From Jesse. From her cousin. From her mother.

A secret that threatens to tear apart Heather's relationship with everyone she cares about.

Continue on in the Moonbeam Bay series and see what the Parker women are up to. And just how many more secrets does this family have?

kaycorrell.com

ISBN 9781944761608

90000

9 781944 761608